CARFAX HOUSE

ALSO BY
SHANI STRUTHERS

CARFAX HOUSE

A CHRISTMAS GHOST STORY

SHANI STRUTHERS

Authors Reach
www.authorsreach.co.uk

ISBN: 978-1-8382204-1-9

Dedication

For Lee, and for Clare. Often thought of with love.

—

Acknowledgements

A huge thank you to my core team of beta readers, Rob Struthers, Kate Jane Jones, Lesley Hughes, Louisa Taylor, and Sarah Savery – your input and enthusiasm for Carfax House was, as usual, invaluable. Big thanks also to Rumer Haven for polishing the manuscript to perfection and to Gina Dickerson of RoseWolf Design for another brilliant cover and formatting. The dream team, here's to the next one…

Chapter One

Carfax House.

Built in 1868 by Simon Lilley, the son of a wealthy Leicestershire landowner and a notable architect in his own right. Constructed with local stone that had weathered from grey to black in places, it had mullioned windows set over two storeys, four on one side of the front door and four on the other, plus the semblance of an archway in which the old oak door stood guard.

I knew from photographs that there was a sweeping staircase to the central hallway that, once upon a time, the host and hostess would descend to meet their guests. I imagined the lady of the house, as grand as the building – grander, even – and the full skirts of her taffeta dress, a soft grey, the colour of a dove, rustling with each step she took. At other times on a day similar to this, icy cold, she might have perhaps stood at one of the ground-floor windows, her mood far more sombre than the sky as eyes searched longingly for a visitor.

Romantic notions, maybe, but a house like this was guilty of inspiring them. In truth, its history was something of a mystery. We'd discovered it on the internet quite by chance. It had been billed as a renovation project, a Victorian country house complete with a few acres of land and all for the price of a London apartment. Grade II-listed, it would take time, money and dedication to restore it to its former standing as one of England's fine houses. A wreck would have perhaps been a more apt way to describe it.

Faced with it at last, and my eyes travelling over every inch from top to bottom and left to right, I noticed several cracked windowpanes and cracked brickwork too, which had, no doubt, allowed the damp in. There was a hole in the red clay tiled roof, and, although a path led up to the house, the front approach resembled a jungle.

I was faced with it, not him. My husband remained in London in surroundings that were luxurious in comparison. Not our apartment in Hammersmith – that was long gone to pay for this – but a hotel room, at least. It was Carfax House that surrounded me now. Sold unseen. At auction. A risk we'd taken, but, as Al said, you have to jump in with both feet sometimes.

Damn! I wished he were here with me, that the murder case he was working on, that could catapult him in his career as a lawyer, was over. It was supposed to be, but these things can lag, the decision to incarcerate someone for life, even if he is as guilty, as arrogant as sin, not to be hurried. Al was thirty-four, two years older than me, and hungry for success. And this impressive country home, albeit aged and neglected, he considered a mark of that.

I remembered our conversation about it. We were both working from home, sitting at opposite ends of the dining table, when he'd lifted his head and called me over.

"Liz, Liz, look at this. See what they're asking for it. Four hundred and fifty thousand pounds, that's all."

I was tapping away on my laptop, writing. That's what I did. I wrote. I was a journalist, working freelance, and throughout my career I had covered many topics. That particular morning, I was researching for an article on how the media perceive and portray women over the age of fifty. Suffice to say, it was in a far from flattering manner, and, although trying to remain unbiased, I was becoming increasingly indignant because of it. Glad of the interruption, I walked over to Al's end of the table to see what he had on his laptop screen.

Carfax House.

A project.

And, yes, it was beautiful. It was…romantic, standing there in such a solemn manner. The photographs had clearly been taken during the winter, as the sky was bleached and leaves had fallen from the copious trees that surrounded the property.

I shook my head. "Too far," I said, beginning to turn away. We were Londoners, born and bred, the pair of us. It's what we knew, where we worked. End of.

Al grabbed my wrist, preventing me from moving further.

"It isn't, though. It's a train ride. Just over an hour and you're in St Pancras. I can easily commute, no problem at all. As for you, you can work anywhere."

I looked into his eyes – they were green with flecks of brown in them, similar to my own – and it was like falling… Not in love. I already loved him. We'd been together ten years and married for five of them. Rather, it was like drowning in excitement. By proxy.

And he knew it.

Confident enough, he released his grip, and I pulled up a chair to sit beside him.

"Show me more."

Several photographs had been taken of the exterior of the house and grounds, several of the inside too, including the entrance hall with that incredible staircase, intricately carved oak newels and oak handrails winding their way upwards. A project. Our project. His and mine. A decade was a long time to be with someone; you had to keep things fresh, and we'd resolved to do that, to keep reinventing ourselves and our lives, never to become…comfortably numb.

"My parents split up because…they couldn't be bothered, basically." He'd told me this early in our relationship, during a drunken night at an Italian restaurant we both liked. "They gave up. Mum's attention strayed, Dad's did too, and that was that. Family life was over, me and my brother travelling between two homes for the rest of our childhood. We can't let what happened to them happen to us, Liz. I don't want to lose you."

"You won't," I'd replied. After all, I, too, knew the pain of separation. "Never."

We hadn't had kids, not yet. We were just too busy, but no doubt about it, we wanted them. Yet another way to reinvent ourselves. Continuing to look at the property online, my mind flitted through the possibility. If we moved out of London, moved somewhere less hectic, to a big enough place – our flat had one bedroom, one *tiny* bedroom – we could think about children, we could plan. A boy and a girl would be the ideal.

Carfax House. Even the name of it sent shivers down my

spine.

"What if it's haunted?" I said, I *blurted* out.

Al tore his eyes from the computer to look at me. For a fraction of a moment, there was silence, and then that silence broke as he burst out laughing.

"Are you serious?"

Actually, I was. I'd always loved words, loved reading; you could say my life had been anchored around both, and maybe, just maybe, my head was too full of Gothic-style classics, the likes of *Jane Eyre, Wuthering Heights, Rebecca* and *Great Expectations*. In books such as those, the house was every bit as much a character as the people, certainly as brooding, its walls the keeper of so many secrets, harbouring the ghosts of those that had lived and died there. And this house, it was so like those that I used to picture in my head, the essence of it. It was lonely. Abandoned. Forgotten.

"How long's it been empty for?" I asked.

"No idea. A while, though, for sure."

"Look it up, see if there's anything about it on the net besides the sales details."

There wasn't, only when it had been built and whom by. Other than that, its past was a deep chasm. One we could fall headlong into if we chose to.

And we did.

We wanted to sell our flat anyway. We'd already talked about moving further to the outskirts, getting something a little bigger with a garden, perhaps. But, come on, this big and with so much land? I was thinking of Ealing! Yet how infectious excitement can be. So we sold our flat – there was a waiting list for our area – and put in a bid. It happened so quickly.

"Like it was meant to be," Al said, his grin transforming him from a man intent on climbing the professional ladder to a schoolboy. I loved it when he smiled like that; I was always happy when he was happy. Aged thirty-four, as I've said, he'd come from a broken home, but it had nonetheless been a good one. He and his brother, Grant, had attended public school, then top universities, acing all exams, falling into the right jobs at the right firms – his brother was an accountant – and both with good looks and charm too. Al was tall with dark hair. I was tall too, with auburn hair. We'd been deemed a good-looking couple by so many, and perfectly suited. With the latter, I agreed. We were *both* ambitious, not just Al, and always busy, even at weekends. Frazzled. This house would give us an opportunity to spend more quality time together, a refuge far from the madding crowds.

And yet here I was, standing in front of it as lonely as the building itself, a nagging fear within me growing more urgent. Yes, the house was an easy enough commute from London. Even so, would it be me here mostly? Rattling around, patching up holes in walls, painting, trying to make it once more into a home – one that our friends could visit and hopefully admire. And when they did, it would be me rather than some faceless heroine sweeping down those stairs, not wearing a taffeta gown, admittedly, but something dazzling, made of silk, perhaps, and emerald green. Al would stand at the bottom, as mesmerised by me as our guests were, congratulating himself all the while on having married me, even though marriage was something he'd declared he didn't believe in. So many times he'd used that old adage: *It's just a piece of paper. An old-fashioned concept.*

Maybe. But I had wanted that commitment. For him to stand up and declare that he loved me in front of everyone, and I'd wanted to do the same. Creating a memory so happy it would obliterate all else. After all, we housed them every bit as much as bricks and mortar did.

I should go inside the house. Not stand here deliberating, remembering…

Just as the photographs I'd seen of the house had been taken on a winter's day, so I saw it now, in winter, the week leading up to Christmas. At home – my old home – in London, the streets would be packed to bursting, people shopping, meeting, celebrating. Like Al, most would be scrambling to bring their work to a reasonable closure before switching off computers and joining in with the festivities. It was a time of year I loved. I would throw myself wholeheartedly into the spirit of the season. But life was different now. We were ready for something else. A new chapter. I wanted to spend Christmas here, with Al, in our new home, not a hotel room.

I should go in. I really should. It was a little after three in the afternoon. If it weren't for horrendous traffic, I would have arrived at least an hour earlier, and daylight wouldn't be retreating already. Before night took hold, I had to unpack the car. I'd brought all the essentials I needed, including a camp bed and heavy duvet. The van with our furniture would be here in the morning, but I wanted to get in first, clean what I could, prepare the ground. That was the plan, *our* plan. But, for Al, at least, the murder case had scuppered that.

Still, just a couple more days and he'd be here. We'd light the fire – there must be several fireplaces to choose from – and settle in, away from the hustle and bustle and away from his family too, most of whom were heading abroad for warmer climes anyway, for Christmas in the sun. And we'd be here, in a house that had once been grand, drinking wine as flames leapt and danced in the grate before us. He'd be grinning again, and so would I. I'd snuggle into his arms and dream about all that this house could be and what it meant for us.

A house caught in perpetual winter. A monument to a bygone age, that stood beneath a bleached sky, soon to be cloaked in darkness. And me alone within.

Carfax House.

What if it's haunted?

Chapter Two

The house was just over an hour's train ride from St Pancras – or, if you were travelling by car as I had, around three hours, depending on traffic – but the countryside was so different. It was rural, I'd expected that, but what I hadn't expected was it to be so sparse. Birmingham, too, was not so far off, an hour's drive west. Leicester was also close. So many towns, so many cities, and yet…Carfax House felt isolated. Removed from society, a world within a world.

The land immediately surrounding me was flat, although there were hills in the distance. And, as I've said, the gardens were junglelike, with overgrown grass, hedges and bushes covered in ivy, weeds as far as the eye could see, and an abundance of trees, some skeletal, some evergreen. They seemed to smother the house, to conspire to keep it alone.

I hurried over to my car and opened the boot. As tempting as it was to go straight to the front door and let myself in, I didn't want to go empty-handed. There was a need in me now to be inside, not out here, exposed – to find a room, a small room, and make it habitable.

The boot was stuffed; there were suitcases and bulging laundry bags too. I grabbed one of those bags as finally, finally, I made my way closer to the house and prepared to enter.

It wasn't the impending darkness outside that spurred me on but the mist too. As the sun set, an ethereal cloud rose, reminding me a little of a spectacle I'd seen before in Iceland, the Northern Lights. Al and I loved travelling, and Iceland had been high on our list of places to see. We'd gone there for a long weekend, followed the usual tourist route, seen the geysers, the waterfalls, the volcanic mountains, and the lights. Regarding those, we'd joined a tour, gone chasing around for them, our guide as desperate as us to find them, to leave his customers satisfied. We'd climbed a hillside late at night, our feet sinking deep into the snow, and it was cold, it was bitter, so much so that some couldn't hack it and had turned back, opting for the warmth of the coach instead, despite the money they'd paid to witness such a phenomenon. But I'd continued, as had Al and two women from Tennessee. We'd climbed that hill, and, on a promise, stood there. That promise was delivered. The mists rose, gradually, artfully, upwards from the ground. They started to sway, to dance, to concertina across the sky. Not coloured lights, not green like we'd expected, just mist, white mist, but it had been magical even so. Spiritual. This mist, here at the house, the way it rose so quickly and spread so widely, blanketing everything – the trees, the ground, the house itself – was a phenomenon too but with one difference: it felt more eerie than spiritual.

As I passed beneath the archway, I shivered. The key to the door was in my coat pocket. Placing the laundry bag on the ground, which was littered with some stones and twigs that I kicked out of the way, I retrieved the key. A big key, heavy, rusting and awkward.

I thought I'd struggle, that I would need both hands to turn it, but the door yielded easily enough, almost as if – damn my imagination and the books I'd immersed myself in over the years – it had been waiting for me. As if it was desperate for company.

Forgetting the laundry bag for the moment, I entered. At the forefront of my mind was the image of the entrance hall I'd seen in the property details. Now I was about to encounter it for real.

The stairway, its treads bare, the balustrade covered in dust, swept upwards, exactly as it had in the photograph. The floor on which I stood was wooden, herringbone parquet, but chipped, uneven and blackened in places. The walls around the staircase were wood panelled, but elsewhere they were plain, perhaps white once upon a time, now grey.

I tipped my head, looked up, and as I did, I gasped. The ceiling wasn't plain. Far from it. Just as the staircase newels were intricately carved, the ceiling was too, a central star with circles and swirls lovingly crafted, a thing of beauty. Or it would be once restored. A light fitting hung there, a chandelier, not glittering but looking sorry for itself, many of its crystals missing. In fact, as I stepped forward, my foot crunched on a fragment that littered the floor. The crack was so loud. No matter. All that mattered was if the light worked.

My eyes searching for switches, I found a panel of them to the left of the oak door. Heading over to it, I swept my hand down several of them, and there was light. Relief swamped me from head to foot. I wouldn't be floundering in the darkness.

I'd left the laundry bag outside but now rushed back to get it, to bring it in, dumping it on the floor beside me, spinning round and around, committing to memory the first sight of our new home. To the right of me, a narrow corridor led to more rooms, the same to the left. I wanted to run suddenly, along those corridors, and begin the exploration. From being trepidatious, I was excited again, swinging wildly between different emotions. But the car, I had to unpack it, and only then could I close the door behind me. Truly enter this world.

Half an hour later and it was done, the hallway littered with my belongings. I was in situ, the sole occupant of a big old, lonely house in the countryside. Tomorrow, the removal team would be here, and the day after that there'd be Al. Coming home for Christmas.

But for now, there was just me.

I ventured to the left first, eyes scanning for more light switches as I walked. It was growing darker outside. And it was dark inside too, pools of black everywhere. And the silence…I wasn't used to it, not coming from London. Even on the journey here there'd been sound, playlists on Spotify blasting various tunes, and me singing along at the top of my voice, loving that there was no one to wince that I was doing so or, as Al would do, make a show of covering his ears with his hands, insisting I was torturing him. But here, in this house, there was only silence. After getting my bearings, I needed to find my beloved and battered Roberts radio, thankful I'd had the presence of mind to pack it as an overnight essential. I'd leave it on for background noise, all night if needs be. It was strange, but as I continued to walk, I fancied such quiet could send you insane.

I pushed open one of the many doors in this corridor and sought the light switch. A living room came into view, empty but with the most gorgeous windows, their sandstone surrounds slightly arched. There was a fireplace too, as I knew there would be, and another chandelier. The boards beneath my feet would need sanding and varnishing, possibly replacing. The walls, as predicted, looked damp in places. It'd be all right, though. We had savings, and both of us earnt a good salary. We could afford to do this, had already agreed we wouldn't rush, that it was a project to handle with care.

Another room that I came upon had a rear view, not that I could see what was out back, not with the night and the mist. A third door revealed a wood-panelled room that was so dark, even with the light on. Beautiful, though – a library, perhaps, or it would be. One more door to try, this one, disappointingly, revealing nothing but a cupboard. Deep, though, great for storage. The kitchen must have been on the other side, so I retraced my footsteps to the entrance hall, not turning off lights, not until I'd decided where I would camp tonight.

There was more living space, certainly, including a room considerably larger than the others, that could have been an entertainment space in the past, severely worn wood beneath my feet perhaps a confirmation of that. At last I found the kitchen, which was huge, a scullery leading off it, as well as a cloakroom with a toilet and washbasin.

A previous owner had installed electric bar heaters, ugly things that looked totally out of place in a house such as this, but I was eager for them to work. Switching a few on, I waited for them to crank themselves up, to lend at least a vestige of warmth.

It was as cold in here as it was on the outside, my breath also becoming misty.

Back in the kitchen, the taps at the butler sink were as rusted as the house key. When I turned one on, it gave a violent shudder before spewing out water that was somewhere between orange and brown. Eventually, it ran clear, and I bent my head to drink, realising how thirsty I was, but the taste was sour. I'd have to dig out the kettle I'd brought and boil the water before drinking any more, try to put aside any thoughts of the lead content from the pipes. The cupboards that lined the walls were plain, fashioned from a dark hardwood. Inside, only dust littered the shelves, nothing more, not even a stray grain of rice. There was an old white enamelled Belling electric cooker, another relic from a bygone age. Apart from that, the house was empty. Completely.

I needed to pick a room, get it cleaned, clean the kitchen too. It might have been plain, but it was serviceable. Hard to say when it had been fitted – at a guess I plumped for the eighties. And it truly was a guess, as there was no nod towards fashion at Carfax House, none at all. Beneath my feet there was no lino but flagstones, and, again, the walls were white.

Which room, then? Which one was the most…welcoming? The least damp. The one I could warm with a plug-in heater I'd also packed, that I'd invested in for this very reason?

The smallest room, of course, just off the kitchen – a study in another lifetime, perhaps, which I could also make my study, the perfect place to sit and write. I could envision it so well: me on an old captain's chair, its leather seat stuffed with horsehair, at a wide desk with a green leather baize. In front of me would be my laptop, a fancy Tiffany-style lamp to lend some colour, my mobile and a few favoured photographs. Now and then, I would lift my head and turn towards the window, stare out at the garden, at land that belonged to no one but us, grounds that stretched onwards towards the distant hills.

I'd set up there and then call Al and let him know I'd arrived. I would have done that before now, but he was in court until five and couldn't be disturbed.

Reentering the entrance hall, I also made plans to dust and scrub what I could and to sweep the floors. All while the radio played. I'd fall exhausted into bed later that evening and sleep soundly until morning, when I'd have more time to get extra cleaning done before the furniture arrived. Oh, the Christmas tree! Where would I put that?

The thought made me smile. The living room with the fireplace, perhaps, by those beautiful arched windows? I'd decorate it before Al got here, hanging from its branches plenty of soft, glowing lights. Gather wood too so that the fire was lit, a bottle of red wine warming beside it and two gleaming glasses ready to be filled.

I knew what I was doing; I was setting the scene, turning a dream, a bold gesture, into reality. *Jumping in with both feet.* Fearless. Determined. Brave. Selling it to myself.

This was his idea, but I had taken little persuading.

I had to remind myself of that, standing there beneath the broken chandelier. I'd readily agreed. And I loved it. I did. The prospect of a renovation excited me. I could blog about it, every step of the way. That kind of thing was very popular nowadays. I could write piece after piece about the 'Escape to Carfax House'. It might not have the same ring as *Escape to the Chateau*, a TV programme I loved, but it still had a certain appeal.

I smiled again, but the smile didn't linger.

Slowly, inevitably, I turned towards the staircase.

I'd explored the downstairs, but there was still the upstairs to go.

It wouldn't take long, just a quick look around, turning on more heaters.

And yet I'd already decided to sleep downstairs.

Why? There were six bedrooms here, according to the details. Six!

I swallowed as I continued to gaze ahead at darkness that seemed to creep down the stairs, easily consuming what light existed.

I shook my head. No.

I wouldn't explore upstairs. Not today.

There was enough to do on the ground floor.

I'd do it tomorrow, when the removal men arrived.

Again, I cursed the case that Al was working on, the murder that kept him from me. If he were here, we'd have no hesitation. Straight after completing the downstairs, we'd run upstairs, choose the best bedroom for ourselves, mark out which one would be ideal as a nursery and which ones our friends and family could sleep in when they visited.

We'd squeal like kids, our heads thrown back with laughter.

But he wasn't here.

I was alone.

Quite alone.

And the darkness, the shadows, continued to creep.

Chapter Three

Much better! The radio was blaring classic Christmas songs, George Michael, David Essex, Slade and Mariah Carey the usual culprits. I never would've had this channel on normally, and certainly not if Al were here. Al liked what he called 'proper music.' Fair enough. I liked and appreciated real music too, but there was room for everything, and these old favourites (of mine, at least) helped to lift the atmosphere, make it lighter when, before, it had settled like a stone. Just as I'd done in the car on the journey here, I sang along at the top of my voice, intent on waking this slumbering giant.

It was convenient that the study was by the kitchen. I could drag my bags towards it, leaving most outside in the corridor, and fetch also the heater I'd brought, plugging it in as a matter of priority, hoping the chill that pervaded this place wasn't overly stubborn. Central heating. We'd budgeted for a new system. As well as our savings, Al's father was helping us out with costs, although he thought we were mad to take the house on.

"You'll regret it," he'd said. "And you'll find it hard to sell on. The previous owner has, hence why it's at auction. They want shot of it. It'll be a money pit."

"I love it, Dad," had been Al's reply. "Me and Lizzie

both."

His dad had softened somewhat. "I know you do, son, and I'll help, you know that too, but...who needs a big house like that nowadays? They cost a fortune to run."

"It's not actually that big," I'd said, eager to defend our decision. "It's six bedrooms, and, well, we do plan to have kids, plus we'll want people to come and stay."

"You do what you want," he'd said, not unkindly, although I was sure I had heard him add something as he'd turned away. "God knows, I've made enough mistakes in my lifetime."

This wasn't a mistake. We'd jumped in with both feet, and we had to make it work.

As I cleaned and scrubbed and swept, I pushed away any further doubts that niggled. I didn't have a clue about interior design, nor did Al. Our flat in London, like this place, was mainly painted white. It was clean, and it was comfortable. We both loved art, and we'd invested in a number of pieces, prints mostly, limited editions. They brought colour, and we adored them, particularly ones that reminded us of places we'd visited: Vestrahorn Mountain in Iceland, scenes of Wales by John Knapp-Fisher, and little Cornish vignettes. For this house, we'd need more pictures; we'd need a mountain of them! But they could be collected over time, accumulated with care.

As for furniture, we'd need plenty more of that too, but, again, I looked forward to touring antique shops, finding unusual items and slowly filling every room with pieces that we'd come to treasure. In fact, earlier when I'd finally spoken to Al, I'd talked about just that – furniture and what would go where. He'd chatted somewhat, excited too, but I could tell he was preoccupied. This case of his, a stabbing – the two young men involved barely twenty years old apiece, one in the dock and one in the ground – it was taking its toll. I let him go, but not before telling him to get enough rest, that I couldn't wait to see him.

After ending the call, my mind wandered back to the décor and the repairs needed. I'd already spotted a hole in the roof that would have to be seen to, and quick. I would look for it in the morning when I ventured upstairs, pop my head into the attic, praying it was recent damage and that the repercussions weren't too hideous.

Holes in roofs, broken tiles, floorboards that needed replacing, damp walls… For a moment as I was standing in the hall, broom in hand, the radio still blaring from the kitchen, I felt overwhelmed. A wave of negativity as unexpected as it was harsh.

Sold unseen. What had we been thinking?

We'd invested our life in the unknown.

My eyes stung, tears pricking at them.

Stop this, Liz! What's done is done.

This is your house now.

Yours.

You're meant to be here.

It's fate.

Fate?

Oh, that was going too far!

I forced a smile as, once more, my eyes travelled to the staircase, imagining what the treads would look like once polished. The newels would also have their finish carefully restored, the spindles repaired where broken and the handrail buffed until it shone as bright as a conker. A grand staircase, a real feature – this entire entrance hall was, with its beautiful ceiling. And so different to what I was used to. In the London flat there'd been no staircase. In the house I'd lived in as a child, there'd been one, but with thirteen steps in total, narrow and steep. And now there was this! A staircase fit for Scarlett O'Hara!

I not only smiled, I laughed. Such dreams! Such fantasies.

Any negative feelings began to disperse.

On the radio, Chris Rea was belting out 'Driving Home for Christmas'.

Which Al would be doing soon, or, rather, the train would whisk him here.

It was me who'd driven home for Christmas.

Home.

Leaning on the broom slightly, I continued to gaze at the stairs.

I'd imagined walking down them a thousand times.

But I had yet to walk up.

* * *

What had I been worrying about?

Upstairs was fine. Absolutely fine. What I'd seen of it.

There had been little time to explore, to open every door and linger, not with the removal men rushing around, asking me what boxes went where and rebuilding some stuff that had been flat-packed. I'd managed to pick out our bedroom, at least, the master bedroom, it looked like, although, to be honest, they were all pretty sizeable. This one, though, had taken my fancy immediately. Positioned in the middle of the house – at the front, above the entrance hall – it was a perfect square with a moulded, albeit cracked ceiling.

I'd also got a good look at the garden to the rear from the landing window. Just as I was no interior designer, I was no gardener either, but I could learn on both counts, me *and* Al. We could have a wildflower section, a place for bees to hover, as well as a more cultivated area and a vegetable patch. I loved the idea of growing my own food.

Whilst still gazing at the garden, I then wondered what it would look like in March, when spring would surely lend it some colour. Right now it was…drab. That was the only way I could think to describe it. The sky was still bleached and the mist hadn't quite dispersed.

It was easy to doubt it ever would.

"Almost done, Liz. A couple more boxes to go."

My reverie, my *unease*, was interrupted by one of the removal men, Dave.

I turned to face him. "That was quick work!"

"Well, there wasn't that much furniture, to be honest," Dave replied, a little ruefully, perhaps. "There are whole rooms that lie empty still. How you going to fill this place?"

"Slowly," I said, smiling.

Leaving the landing, I walked with him downstairs and towards the kitchen, where my bag was. Also now situated in there was the table that Al and I would eat and work at in the flat. It seemed so small, so…inadequate. Clearly, Dave thought so too.

"It's quite a task you've taken on," he remarked.

"I'm aware."

"Lonely spot."

"It's certainly that."

"And your husband's arriving tomorrow?"

"Uh-huh. He'll finish work, then catch the train here."

"In time for Christmas, eh?"

"Absolutely."

"So, you'll be all right 'til then?"

I laughed, but inwardly this time. If I said, 'No, I don't think so,' what would he say to that? Would he offer to stay with me? He and his men, protecting the little woman. "I really am okay," I said and then, unable to resist, added, "Why so worried?"

Dave coloured a little. "It's a big place to be on your own, that's all. Gonna get a dog?"

"A dog?"

"Yeah, this place could do with a dog."

"Someone to guard me?"

He coloured some more.

I relented. "I might well get a dog in the future. We'd like to have kids too."

"Bring the place to life."

"Exactly."

"That's what it needs. Some life."

"It does. It's been empty a long time."

"Dave!" one of his men called. "That's it, last box sorted."

Dave turned, shouted in acknowledgement and then looked straight back at me. In his fifties, he was short but stocky with broad shoulders, the ideal build for his profession. Not particularly handsome, he nonetheless had kindness in his face…and concern.

"Dave—" I began, but he cut across me.

"Just don't seem right, that's all."

"What doesn't?"

"To leave you here."

"It's my home!" I couldn't quite hide the amusement in my voice. "And, as I've told you, I won't be alone for long. Look, it's sweet of you to be so concerned, I really do appreciate it, but... Do you come from a big family?" I had the sudden impression he did.

He nodded, surprised I'd asked.

"One you're going home to very soon?"

"We're working tomorrow, and then that's it. We're downing tools for the holidays."

"Nice," I said. "I hope you'll have a wonderful time. And I will too, right here, setting things up, setting the Christmas tree up as well. I may be alone for now, but I'm not lonely, not one bit." Because he still didn't seem convinced – indeed, his eyes flickered slightly to the left and to the right – I found myself confiding in him. "I don't come from a big family. My father...he...um...left us, when I was young. It's the same old, same old, I'm afraid. He had an affair, found someone else. It was just me and Mum when I was growing up, and she had to work hard in order for us to live comfortably. Relatively comfortably, anyway. I grew used to spending time on my own. I loved to write. That's what I do. I'm a journalist. I loved to read as well. I can amuse myself, no problem, and, believe me, there's plenty to keep me entertained here: cleaning, house repairs, the garden. Being alone doesn't faze me."

Why all these words, these pacifications, these *justifications*, were spilling from me, I didn't know. I just...didn't want to be worried about it, I suppose. Al wasn't worried; I'd phoned him earlier to tell him the removal men had got here. Again, he could only speak briefly. He was due in court and also worried about the murder charge being reduced to manslaughter. He had a lot on his mind.

There was another bout of silence between Dave and me, and then gradually, by increments, he relaxed, his shoulders sagging when before they'd been rigid.

"Best get going," he said. "Get back to London before the hell of rush hour."

"Sure," I said, glancing at my watch. It was barely past one o'clock. They should make it. Just. "I'll see you out." And I'd sort out a tip for them too; they'd been so helpful.

A few minutes later, having grabbed my purse, I pushed a few notes into his hand.

"Seriously," I said, trying to quash any objection, "you've worked hard."

As his team filed out and clambered into the van, he spoke again. "I hope you have a happy Christmas," he said, and I couldn't return the sentiment. I could only nod.

The reason?

Because despite his well wishes, there was only sadness in his voice.

Chapter Four

The bed was in place upstairs, freshly made up. I'd unpacked some clothes and put them in the wardrobe, and I'd scattered a few ornaments over various surfaces in order to give it a more homely feel. There were no curtains at any of the windows, but that could hardly be considered a dealbreaker, as I wore an eye mask in bed anyway. I could pass the night in here easily enough, but the study downstairs…the bed was made up there too, and it was less cold, almost warm in comparison to up here, where, yes, despite more electric heaters having been turned on, the chill was proving stubborn indeed. I might as well stay downstairs, I reasoned, just until Al arrived. I didn't want to sleep in the bed without him, not really. That truly would be a case of me rattling around!

I headed back downstairs, and the day passed quickly enough.

I phoned Al again; he had more time for me on this occasion.

"So, it's looking good, is it?" he asked.

"It is. Spartan, but…you know…"

"It's spartan for now. Come the new year, we'll go shopping."

"Our year," I breathed, my hand travelling towards my stomach. Perhaps it would be special in more ways than one. "So, I take it there's no way you can get here tonight."

"Nope, sorry, we're still waiting on the jury."

"But tomorrow you can."

"Hopefully."

"Hopefully?" I quizzed, picking up on the hesitation in his voice.

"The verdict's due this afternoon, but I've a feeling the jury will ask for more time."

"They're cutting it fine, aren't they? It'll soon be Christmas Eve."

"Oh, it'll be done and dusted by then."

"I feel sorry for him, you know, facing life imprisonment at such a young age."

"At least he's got a life still, unlike the boy he's stolen life from."

Gangs. London was full of them. So many incidents like this happening day in, day out, some making the papers, some not. The speeding, unmarked grey vehicles of armed response practically a daily sight. There'd been a bit about this case in the nationals, but only a few lines; it was just too commonplace to warrant more. Perhaps it really was for the best that we got out of London, which was changing rapidly. It was no place to bring kids up, as Al had previously pointed out. "We need to leave while we can," he'd said.

"I'm excited to see you," I continued, changing the subject. "For you to see this place."

"Is it everything we've dreamed of?"

"It's all of that and more. It's going to be fantastic, Al, it really is. Oh, and if you pass a newsagent, can you pop in and pick up every interiors magazine going?"

"Will do. What's mobile reception like up there?"

"A bit patchy, but that's to be expected. I've been on the phone to the internet guys today. They're coming on the twenty-ninth to connect us to the outside world."

I could almost see the wistful smile on Al's face. "Seems a shame, doesn't it, that we have to connect, although at the same time it's vital if we're going to work there."

"It does," I agreed. Having put work on hold until the new year, I was looking forward to a hiatus from social media, from Facebook, Twitter, Insta, from emails flooding in about work, although I acknowledged I was lucky to have plenty of work in the offing. I still wanted time to create that blog, though, to chart our progress with the renovation, and maybe, just maybe, one day I might sit in my new study and write a novel of my own. It was a quiet ambition, the prospect of 90,000 words-plus a little daunting, but nothing ventured, nothing gained. Feature Carfax House, why not? *What could I write about you?*

"You sure you don't want me to WhatsApp photos?" I asked. I'd offered on my first night here – certainly, I'd taken loads – but his answer was the same now as it had been then.

"I want to see it with my own eyes."

After the phone call, I'd gone out into the garden, letting myself out via the door from the scullery. This weather! Cold, grey and misty, it was relentless. I'd asked Al how the weather was in London – cold but crisp, he'd said, one of those winter days that I loved. When he'd said that, I experienced the first pang of longing for the life I'd so recently given up. If I were there today, I'd head to one of the parks, St James's, with its lake and fountains and my favourite bridge, crunching leaves underfoot, taking nuts to feed the squirrels and bread for the birds.

There should be plenty of wildlife to spot here too, hiding beneath the hedgerows. I could always leave some nuts and bread out for them. But, oh, the work this garden was going to need! As much as the house, that was for sure. Perhaps we should hire a power scythe – that would make lighter work of all the cutting back – plus get one of those mowers you sat on. That would be fun. It was difficult to venture too far into the garden; I had boots on, but they were only soft leather. I'd need sturdy Wellingtons or walking boots to stomp my way through this. Dripping in mist. That's what it seemed to be. A garden lost in time, lost to the world.

Left to rot.

A shiver ran through me. The temperature dipped.

I should choose my words more carefully.

This garden wasn't rotting. It was flourishing still, despite everything. All it needed was love and care. Something it hadn't seen for a long time.

How long?

We'd bought this house, it was ours, and yet, as I've said, we only knew the basics about it. Not because we hadn't tried to find out, we had, but there was nothing about it on the net. No information other than the year it had been built and the architect, who'd built several houses in Leicestershire and neighbouring counties, apparently, and had been a big name in his day. What notable family had commissioned him to build it? The Carfax family, for whom the house was named? I'd tried to find some evidence of them too but, again, without success. What other families had come after? More to the point, why had they left?

I spun around to face the house, a sudden action, as if my body knew something my mind had yet to acknowledge. Had I heard something? Something out of the ordinary?

I stood there, just as I'd stood the day before, but this time staring at the rear of the house rather than the front. A simple, flat elevation, the walls were similarly blackened in places, with windows like blind eyes.

My eyes travelled to each window from left to right, starting with those downstairs, then rising to scan the windows above. The three bedrooms that overlooked the rear would most likely be guest bedrooms, the three at the front kept for family.

Lifting my gaze, the roof on this side of the house was fairly intact, only a few roof tiles missing and dislodged, the casualties of some storm, perhaps, and the guttering a bit wrecked in places, as was to be expected. And then, again, seemingly of its own volition, my gaze returned to the bedroom on the far right and settled there. More shivers coursed through me, the mist that surrounded me pooling like the darkness pooled inside, like the shadows did too, my feet in my soft leather boots beginning to burn with cold.

Had I heard a noise, or had I sensed something else? Movement?

In that room, on the far right.

Is that why I had turned so hastily?

A window there, not the main bedroom window but one

next to it, small and oval, a bit of a quirky feature and one that wasn't mirrored on the other side of the house.

There was no movement, not at that small window or elsewhere, although I scanned and scrutinised each pane.

None at all.

* * *

Once again, sleep came easily.

I had returned inside after my foray into the grounds, shaking my head at how wild my imagination was running, part amused, part bemused by it. I was right about something, though. This house was inspirational, that novel I dreamt of writing – something wild and romantic – coming to fruition, perhaps, alongside other hopes and aspirations.

Downstairs, I continued to unpack boxes and position ornaments, tried also to get the TV set up properly but failed, making me appreciate the Roberts radio even more. On and on it played throughout the evening, background noise, sometimes music, sometimes chatter between a presenter and his guest, a comforting hum. I hoovered up dust, spiders and flies from windowsills, and cobwebs from corners, that had grown dark and stringy. For dinner, I rustled up a little pesto pasta, resolving to find the nearest decent supermarket and go shopping soon, and boiled more water to drink. We'd have to find a local plumber, find out why the water tasted so sour. Good God, I hoped there was nothing dead in the pipes, nothing…decaying.

Al would be here tomorrow, late, after the working day was finished. He'd catch the train and I'd drive to the station to meet him. I'd get all our favourites in beforehand, the foods of the season, and wine too. We could then batten down the hatches, not venture out until Christmas was over. Really get a feel for the house, its nooks and crannies.

By the time it was ten o'clock, I was exhausted, wiped out.

Little wonder sleep came easily.

I hunkered down in the study, cosy, warm and content. How lucky Al and I were to have this house, to have each other and a future laid out before us, one that was good and solid, and bursting with opportunity. I was practically tingling with contentedness, a smile on my lips as I popped my eye mask on, the radio still on but down low.

I slept for hours, deeply, not dreaming as far as I can remember. Then I awoke. I was thrown out of sleep, yet morning was still such a long way off.

"Damn," I whispered, removing my eye mask, wondering why I'd woken. Again, had I detected movement of some sort? Elsewhere in the house. A thought crossed my mind, a terrifying one. Could it be rats running across floorboards and rafters, the scampering of tiny feet? I hated rats. Rodents of any kind, really. Shit! Of course a place like this would have rats! Why hadn't I considered that beforehand? Why hadn't it even crossed my mind when Al had first brought this place to my attention? It had stood empty for…I wasn't sure how long, but a considerable period of time, that much I was certain of. And another thing I knew: when people moved out, other things moved in, spiders and flies, both of which I could deal with. But rats!

Oh, Al, you'd better be here tomorrow! You can deal with this. Get pest control in to clear the place.

It might not be rats, though.

I strained my mind for a memory of what I might have heard. A thump? A scrape?

I focused so hard it took a while to register something else.

There was no low hum from the radio, no tinkle of music or low voices chatting. There was nothing, only silence.

What the hell?

What had happened to the radio?

I threw my duvet off and rose from the camp bed, which hadn't proven as comfortable a second night running, as my side was aching. The room was no longer warm either, cold despite the plug-in and electric heaters. I exhaled and saw how my breath misted once again in front of me, a white cloud that took its time to disperse. Looking over at the window, it was also white outside. *Snow?* I moved closer. No. Nothing as festive as that. It was the mist. A thick wall of it, the kind you might expect to encounter in the Highlands of Scotland, where it's nature that prevails, but here in Leicestershire? A county just over an hour's train ride from London. But then, hadn't London suffered some real pea-soupers in its time, caused by a combination of industrial pollution and high-pressure weather conditions? The former couldn't be responsible here, but the latter…

Snow would be so much better than mist. Snow would be…joyful. Just imagine if mine and Al's first Christmas here was a white one! It would add to the magic.

But there was no magic tonight, only darkness, coldness, mist and silence.

What was it that had pulled me from sleep?

Because something had.

33

I'd woken with such a start, breathless almost.

What if it wasn't rats responsible but people instead? An intruder of some sort.

To be honest, when I had first entered this house, I'd been surprised. Not by the state of it…I'd expected that. But I'd thought I would also see some graffiti on the walls, the handiwork of teens who'd known there was an abandoned house nearby and had broken in and partied. Maybe that had indeed happened. Maybe those who'd handled the sale of the house had come in beforehand and swept away bottle after broken bottle of vodka and, worse still, needles. Given the walls a bit of a scrub, preparing it for sale, as eager as the owners to offload it. But I didn't think so. Not very likely. The loneliness that clung here was just too entrenched. No one had come near Carfax House for a long, long time. Again, I wondered about its history and the name of the individual we'd bought it from, Thomas Lint. Which was mostly the sum total of what I knew about him. The auction house had handled everything, the estate agents and the solicitors, certain words not spoken but nonetheless resoundingly clear: *The house is a steal. It's a bargain. Don't question why.*

Perhaps we shouldn't have jumped in feet first, been more cautious.

Something else resounded, stopping any further musings.

An echo.

Just that.

Coming from inside. But far off.

An echo of what?

A whisper, was that it?

Could a whisper produce an echo?

I should go and see. It was 3.30 a.m., however, and I didn't want to. I wanted to sleep. Wake when morning arrived, when there might still be mist but there would also be light.

I needed the light.

I craved it.

But sleep wouldn't come. Only thoughts that plagued me.

One in particular. *What if it's haunted?*

Chapter Five

There was electric light, at least. And I would make good use of it. I could do what I'd done before and flick every light switch and leave them all blazing. My house, my electricity bill. I'd just have to deal with it, write a little extra to pay a bigger bill. Who cared? Needs must.

Rising from bed, I slipped into the corridor. Unable to bear the thought of cold, bare wood beneath my feet, I'd pulled on my boots and also my dressing gown.

I was no breathless female, no scaredy-cat. I could do this, sort my own problems out. But, oh, the temptation to get on the phone to Al, to wake him up and ask for advice! It would be unfair to do that, though. He needed his sleep too. Plus, being so far away and unable to get to me straightaway, he'd only worry. He hadn't made me come here ahead of him; that had been my idea. As soon as we'd known he would be delayed by work, we could have rescheduled the moving date to the new year and stayed on at the hotel. But I'd refused – I wanted to be in by Christmas, get our new life off to a good start. And even Al didn't work on Christmas Day. He'd be here in time, no question about it. Now, though, I was questioning the wisdom of my insistence. I felt...vulnerable.

God, the darkness in the corridor was as much a physical barrier as the mist. I had to walk a few steps into it to reach the light switch, cursing that I'd closed the study door behind me. If it were open, some light would have spilled out and guided the way, but what was done was done, and so on I walked, as quickly as I could, both my hands held out.

Like being blind.

Like being lost.

Like being…

Liz, stop it! Get a hold on yourself!

Like being dead. That had been my next thought. I berated myself for it – quite rightly – but, even so, I grabbed my wrist to check for a pulse.

Like being imprisoned.

Light. At last!

Powerful enough to chase away any lingering stupidity.

Reaching the panel in the entrance hall, light flooded that too. I wished it would continue up the stairwell, but it didn't. I wished it because that's where the whispers had come from.

Still in the entrance hall, I contemplated crossing over to the left side of the house, to turn the lights on there. But what was the point? It was empty there. And so dark. Pools now solidifying. And yet it wasn't dark outside; it was white. The mist pushed up against the windows, something in it, perhaps, like Cathy from *Wuthering Heights*, a ghostly figure, a crack in her voice as she pleaded, *Let me in! Let me in!*

There were cracked panes in the house, several of them. Would the mist drift in through those? Until the house became smothered in it. Until I was?

"Stop this!"

I issued the command through gritted teeth.

If I was to continue living here, being alone on occasions when Al had to overnight in London, I had to rein in my imagination. Although, in fairness, there was nothing to stop me from overnighting in London with Al too. Most hotel rooms had twin or double beds. But that would defeat the object. I couldn't keep running. This was our house. Our furniture, our paintings, all the things we loved. It wasn't quite a home, not yet, but it would be.

I hadn't tackled the upstairs my first night here, but on this night – what was left of it – I would. Break the spell, the grip that fear had on me like thumbscrews, tightening.

With renewed determination, I climbed the staircase. The light switch for the landing was positioned at the top. We'd need to rewire, include a switch downstairs that flooded the stairs from top to bottom. It was just another thing on the to-do list, my heart trying to remain buoyant as that list stretched on and on, remembering other lists made at this time of year: Christmas lists. I used to write those too, as a kid, and they'd stretch for eternity, all the things that I'd wanted, that I'd wished so hard for. After a certain age, it hadn't always been toys or books or videos. Lists that I'd have destroyed rather than show Mum.

Whilst on the top tread, my hand reached out yet again. Rather than ceiling lights, there were wall sconces, fancy to look at but wholly ineffective. I switched them on, and there was light but not much, some sconces flickering, causing my heart to flicker too.

Silence. Not even the hoot of an owl from outside. And

just as the darkness had coagulated downstairs, so did the mist outside. There were gardens out there, there was land – civilisation was but a short drive away – and yet here I was, suspended.

What time was it now? When would dawn break? When would there be some relief?

I continued walking. There were bedrooms to the left and right, my bedroom too, where I should be, not hiding in the study. I'd peeked into the others, but little more than that. Now, though, I had to do better, starting with the rooms to my left, flooding each with light and scanning every corner. They were big old, vacant rooms, begging for love and attention. I had to check cupboards too, in-built, flimsy things, no sturdier than cardboard, which I'd already decided had to be ripped out. Door after door was flung open.

There was nothing and no one.

The bathroom was next, another vast room, and not one I'd made use of yet, preferring to wash in the downstairs cloakroom instead. There was a bath at one end, complete with clawed feet and a rolled top. A beautiful bath, an antique, but it would need hardcore restoration to remove the limescale that had built up where the tap had dripped, and there was dirt around the edges too, ingrained. The toilet had a pull chain, quaint, but it would no doubt make a racket when pulled. The toilet lid was down, and I was grateful for that, seeing in my mind's eye brown, sludge-like water that might lie at the bottom of it.

All that mattered was it was empty.

I stood again at the door to my bedroom and looked in. It was actually quite inviting. The windowpanes were all intact, and the light was bright enough courtesy of a single bare bulb. Perhaps I'd stay up here until morning, get myself used to it.

Three rooms and the bathroom done, three more to go.

All was quiet. No noise at all.

In yet another bedroom, I walked boldly over to the built-in wardrobe and, as I'd done previously, yanked open the doors. There was no masked marauder waiting to spring forward, only the smell of damp, as sour as the water that pumped through the veins of this house, peeling wallpaper on the inside surfaces, and droppings on the floor. Mouse droppings. Or rats. We'd definitely need pest control. Set traps everywhere. Get rid of them.

The fifth bedroom was opposite. The door was closed, but I opened it, the sconce beside me not just flickering but hissing. I turned towards it, wanting to wrench the bulb from its socket, preferring the quiet to the buzz. Wary of being electrocuted, I resisted.

Empty. Again. Only the begging mist at the windows.

The sixth bedroom was the last one to check, and then I'd be done. I'd return to bed. Not up here but in the study, where I was all set up. I'd shut my eyes, turn the radio back on and, if not sleep fully, then doze at least. I wondered about the radio. Was there something wrong with it? It was certainly old, a present to myself around twelve years ago. I'd always wanted one. I should replace it, really, or take it somewhere and get it repaired.

This was the room with the quirky little window, which I'd only noticed from the outside. What was wrong with me? I felt breathless as I approached it, had to pause and collect myself. I'd opened the doors to all the other rooms, and I'd closed them all behind me. This door, however, was ajar. If I'd peeked in earlier, when the removal men were here, hadn't I closed it behind me? Ordinarily, I would have done. I didn't like doors to be ajar; they had to be either fully open or closed. If I had left it open, however, I couldn't remember. Ajar it was, and from inside darkness was seeping out, just like I imagined the mist seeping in through the windowpanes. Two elements melding, intent on suffocation.

Damn it, but my hand was trembling as my fingers closed around the door handle.

I pushed. Where was the light switch? Where? It should be behind the opening edge of the door, surely?

My hand flailed as I ventured further in. If only I'd brought a torch with me; even the light from my mobile would have sufficed. The light that was behind me, flickering but no longer hissing, seemed to refrain from entering, from lending any support whatsoever. It was only me that entered, and it was so cold that I fancied I could feel the very marrow in my bones crystallise. The windows must have been fractured in here too. It was the only explanation.

Venturing deeper, I kept close to the wall, hands searching all the while.

Where was the light switch?

It was here; it had to be. Every room had them.

Where the hell was it?

Found it! At last.

Christ! Why I'd had trouble, I didn't know. It was exactly where it ought to be.

A bedroom. One I'd only previously peeked into, another

door at the far corner.

I must have spotted this other door before, and yet…I hadn't registered it. Not fully. Got distracted, perhaps, by the removal men, called away.

If there was an intruder, was this their hiding place?

Still trying to control my breathing, I headed towards it. A small door, I'd have to lower my head to enter it. And it looked ancient, older than the house, even, another relic. Made of wood, most likely oak, it was faded in colour, almost as white as the sky, and its surface pockmarked from creatures that had feasted upon it. There was an iron ring that you'd need to push for it to open, the door perhaps creaking, whining and protesting all the while. Hissing. Just like the light in the wall sconce hissed. A warning to keep away.

This was ridiculous! There was no one in the house besides me. I should go downstairs, do as I planned and get more sleep. Come back in the morning, not creep around still.

Exhaustion catching up with me again, my hands rubbed at sore eyes.

Beforehand, I'd urged myself to go forwards; now it was the opposite. I backed away, one step and then another. Was I scared? Maybe. I was just so…unused to this house, to so much space. An abyss. That's what it felt like. I was used to walls closing in on me, to people living only feet away in other flats, the living and the breathing.

Was that someone else's breathing I could hear or my own?

Ragged and full of sorrow.

An echo of something.

From behind the old oak door.

Words being whispered…

No!

Enough!

No more of this!

I turned and fled, retracing my footsteps down the landing with its flickering lights, down the grand, sweeping staircase, then veering towards the study, that echo hissing in my ear now and in my mind. It was every bit as frantic as I was.

Chapter Six

"You're not serious!"

"I'm sorry."

"But the verdict's been agreed, not manslaughter, murder. You won. You got justice. Job done. What's the holdup now?"

"Paperwork. You know how it is."

"Do it here!"

"It's just easier, you know, if I'm in the office. Get it filed properly."

"It's the twenty-second of December!"

"And, technically, still a working day, Liz."

"You worked all last weekend and several weekends before that."

"I'm busy, Liz! This is a big deal for us. You should be proud of me, not shouting at me."

"I need you here."

"Why?"

"*Why?*"

"Liz, is everything all right?"

"What? Um…yes. Why shouldn't it be?"

"You sound…stressed."

My laughter was bitter. I knew it was. "You've no idea

what we've landed ourselves with. This house…the work that needs doing. I don't know if we're up to it."

His laughter was more indulgent. "Not up to it? Al and Liz Greenaway? We bloody well are! We can do anything. We knew it would need work; we'd accepted that."

"It's too big." There, I'd said it. The house was just…too big.

"It won't always be just us in it."

Us? "It's not us, though, is it? It's me and only me. You were supposed to be coming up today, and now you won't because you're too busy. I wanted you to be here."

"Liz" – his voice hardened as his amusement vanished – "I said we should postpone the move until after Christmas, but you wouldn't have it…"

"Precisely because of Christmas! Because…it's a special time. It meant something to me to be here for it. I wanted it to kick-start this new phase in our life, for it to be magical."

"And it will be, Liz, it will be. I'm coming home in plenty of time for Christmas." There was a slight pause. "It's sweet, you know."

"What is?"

"How much you love this time of year, how you always want it to be so special. You're really a big kid inside, aren't you?"

"A big kid? I…don't know about that."

"You are. Look, one more day, okay? That's all. And I'll be there."

"Promise?"

"I promise. So, what will you do today?"

"Um…" I hadn't really thought about it. As soon as I'd woken up, I'd got straight on the phone to Al, needing to hear his voice. Should I mention what had happened a few hours before? I decided not to. I was confused as to whether I really had heard an echo of something, some whispers, or if I'd imagined it all. I had indeed managed to sleep, so I couldn't have been that freaked by it. And this morning, the radio was on low, and the mist had receded. There was even a hint of blue in the sky.

"Liz?" Al prompted.

"I…I'm going to put the Christmas tree up, that's what!" I forced some jollity into my voice. "Go shopping and do some baking."

"The oven works okay?"

"I haven't actually put it to the test, but the hobs do, so fingers crossed. We're going to need an Aga in there, I think, not least for the warmth it chucks out. Oh, and I'm going to tie holly around the bannister. Fresh holly if I can find some. If not, I'll buy fake."

"Sounds like a plan."

"Yeah, yeah. It does."

"Tomorrow will arrive soon enough."

Tomorrow and tomorrow and tomorrow… But he was right; I couldn't berate him any further. This could have all waited a couple of weeks.

We said goodbye. He murmured that he loved me, I said the same, and the call ended. A big kid. Excited. Full of anticipation. Full of…nerves.

Fuck this!

I stood up and took a deep breath. I would not be afraid in my own home. I was going to find out what lay behind that ancient door in the sixth bedroom.

Right now.

Still in my pyjamas, I grabbed my dressing gown, wrapped it around me and put on my boots, just as I'd done in the early hours, and headed back into the corridor to stand there, shivering. The temperature seemed to rise and dip in this house, making it go from just about bearable to bloody freezing. This was one of those bloody freezing moments.

Heading along the corridor, I rubbed my hands together, trying to inject some feeling back into them. I also pledged to rein in any stray thoughts. The door in the sixth bedroom would lead to just another empty room, one with a quirky oval window. It was extravagant wardrobe space, perhaps, or…an en suite. None of the rooms had en suites in this house, not yet, anyway, but maybe a previous owner had installed this one. What I *wasn't* going to find was some blackened cubbyhole with a dead body holed up in it.

I could kick myself for even thinking it.

When I'd fled back to the study last night, I hadn't bothered to turn any lights off upstairs. The sconces in the corridor, to my mind, had made only a slight impression on the darkness, one of them fizzing and hissing at me. As I reached the landing, they were still on, still flickering but intermittently, as if they themselves were exhausted.

Lamps, that's what it needed. We could place antique console tables up here with lamps on them. Just until we got the rewiring sorted. There was a way around everything.

I turned the lights off and continued walking. We'd need several runners too, imported from Iran, perhaps, handwoven by a family sitting around in a circle, swapping tales and talking. A patronising idea, I supposed, but it was better than the ones that wanted to force entry into my

47

mind, so I went with it. Maybe – although I didn't have a talent for crafts – I could sit with my children around the fire come the future, making things too, decorations, for starters. Paper chains. We'd need a ton of them for this house! Again, I idealised the scene, strove to imagine a boy with short, dark hair like Al's and a girl with auburn waves like me. My children's feet would scamper down this landing, and their laughter would fill the rafters. Maybe we'd love being parents so much we'd have more than two – we'd have a small army! It wouldn't always be me alone here. Waiting.

I was at the door to the sixth bedroom. It was ajar like before, which wasn't right. I'd shut it when I'd left it last night; I was absolutely certain of it. I'd slammed it into place.

But it was ajar, *precisely* as it had been in the early hours.

Was subsidence the reason? We'd had a structural report done, however, and no such fault had been noted. Indeed, we'd been impressed by what a sound house this was. Solid. They'd built them well in those days. To last. Maybe it was a weak door latch.

Just go in. Get it over and done with.

I would. I had other things to do today. A dream to pursue.

The room was still cold, but colder than the others? Perhaps. The walls were so damp. Gazing upwards, I saw a stain on the ceiling too, round but jagged, black spots of mould peppered in and around it. I'd noticed a hole in the roof when standing and staring at the front of the house on the day I'd arrived, but that was over the bedroom opposite this. I'd noticed no holes in the roof at the back. Damp was getting in somewhere, though. I should check the attic. A thought that made me shudder. No. No way was I going up there before Al arrived, I decided. My mind was proving too lively for that, instantly recalling *Jane Eyre* and the woman held prisoner in the attic, Rochester's wife Bertha, a woman who was…mad, quite mad. I gulped, felt waves of hot and cold wash over me. Felt anger too, that I was allowing myself to get het up again. Calm. That's normally me. Bobbing along on an even keel. I was happy. And I could be happier still, in this house. So why continue to do this? Terrify myself? Torture myself?

Even so, the attic was a step too far. It also wasn't safe to go up a ladder when there was no one else around. No, it would definitely be Al's job, one of his first, a roof inspection and calls made post-Christmas to those who could do the patching up.

Time to get this over and done with, look behind the door and solve the mystery.

My hand reached out, hesitating only briefly to clasp at the iron ring. It was by far the coldest thing I'd experienced in this house, as if formed of ice, and it was old, so many hands having grasped it through the centuries and now my own. *Come on, Liz, push. Find out what this is. A closet of some sort?*

The door didn't give easily; if anything, it seemed to push right back, wanting to stay exactly where it was, not to have its secrets disturbed, an oak-and-iron protector.

But I had to know.

I pushed, and I pushed, lifted my knee and used that to help me in my efforts.

Gradually it yielded, bit by bit, a creak like a dying

scream.

I gasped as the room beyond was at last revealed.

Not a room. Not exactly. It was far from *just* a room.

* * *

The town was heaving, and the enormous Christmas tree in the centre of it all was beautiful, a true testament to the season, big red velvet bows upon its many branches and baubles everywhere, some of them the size of your head, I swear!

At the foot of the tree was a marketplace, a 'winter village' where people sat in clusters and enjoyed either mulled wine or mugs of hot chocolate, which was also freshly decorated but with cream, marshmallows and red and green sprinkles. It was cold, but there was no mist; the closer I got to town, the more it had receded. The sky was blue, although clouds were gathering.

I had no hot drink to warm me, and nor did I need one. The sight of the tree had warmed me enough, the sheer scale of it, the effort that had gone into making it something to behold, the care that had been taken an inspiration. I'd follow suit, shop 'til I dropped today, buy so many decorations that the suspension on my car would be tested to the maximum. I'd fill that house of mine with festivity. I'd tune in to the Christmas channel on the radio and listen to yet more cheesy tunes. *It's Christm-a-a-s!* Noddy Holder's voice as he belted out this statement in Slade's song 'Merry Xmas Everybody' filled my head. It would be merry. And it would be magical. Was I as big a kid as Al claimed? I wasn't, not really, but there was something about Christmas that drummed up the enthusiasm we all had when we were kids, a zest for life, for fun and games, for something as simple as love. During the darkest season of the year, Christmas reminded us that there was light. Maybe that's what I truly loved about it, what everyone did. That reminder.

First stop: Debenhams.

This town, this city centre, was great. I'd never been to the Bullring in Birmingham before, but it had shops to rival London and an atmosphere that buzzed. There were so many people! As I turned from the tree towards my destination, I was stunned by the crowds. Young people, old people, families and groups of friends were everywhere. It made me bristle slightly, made me a little tense. So many people…and strangers every one of them. Jostling past me, looking straight through me. Like I didn't exist.

The ghost of Carfax House.

Entering Debenhams, I shook my head. What a notion! Plus, when did I get so unused to crowds? I was from London, for God's sake! The most crowded city in the UK. And yet…just two days alone had changed me. So quickly I'd got used to my own company.

"Lovely, aren't they?"

I'd reached the Christmas department in Debenhams and was standing there, idly, once more lost in my own head. It took a moment to register that the person beside me was addressing me. "Sorry? Did you say something?"

It was an old lady, likely in her late seventies, with a puff of white hair and powder congealing in the lines on her face. She had a sweet smile and a light in her faded eyes.

"These baubles," she continued, unabashed. "They're

very colourful."

"Um…yes. Yes, they are."

There were so many baubles laid out before us, boxes and boxes of them, and my eyes had been on some icy blue ones, thinking how they captured the cold, just like the door handle to that room captured it. Her eyes, however, appeared to be travelling all over the brighter ones, the greens, the reds and the golds.

"Thinking of getting some," she said. "Silly, really."

I frowned. "Silly? Why?"

Her smile became tinged with sadness. "There's only me at home, has been for a long while. My husband has passed, my daughter is all grown up – she lives abroad, Australia, no less. Oh, we talk on FaceTime, we talk a lot, but…she has a family of her own, a life of her own. She can't come over for Christmas. It's too expensive, for a start."

"So you won't decorate your house, then?" I asked.

"What's the point? Only me to see it. Christmas is for the little ones." A sigh escaped her. "They're just so pretty, just caught my eye, you know. Maybe I'll get one and hang it from a plant. Got a yucca tree indoors. It can hang from there." She laughed at the thought.

"Choose one," I said. "I'll buy it for you."

Quickly she shook her head "What? Oh no, dear, no. I didn't mean for you to do that. I wasn't looking for a sympathy vote."

"I know, I know," I added just as quickly, wondering too at my offer. "But, really, I'd like to. It's…Christmas, after all. And, yeah, we should all give a nod towards it."

"That's very sweet of you, dear."

"Honestly, it would be my pleasure. Please, choose one."

The older woman paused, probably trying to get the measure of me. But wasn't that what Christmas was all about? Giving to others? Just as suddenly as I'd offered, I was suddenly as desperate for her to accept. Or what? I'd feel like a fool, I supposed. An idiot do-gooder.

The smile was back on the woman's face. "Okay, then. I'll let you buy me a bauble as long as you let me buy you something too."

"No, really, there's no need—"

"I know there isn't, but…you'll be doing me another favour if you accept."

"But—"

"Just a coffee, that's what I meant. There's a café right here, in the store."

"A coffee? Um…okay. Yes, that would be lovely. Thank you. I'd really like that."

"Good," she said, her hand reaching out to pat mine briefly before gravitating to the brightest bauble of them all. Some – the less charitable – might even say the gaudiest.

"I'll have that one, please," she continued.

Chapter Seven

Coffee with Patricia was lovely, the highlight of the day. The highlight of my year, if I was honest. It just left me feeling so…warm inside.

Patricia Brown, aged seventy-eight and really quite sprightly.

I bought her the bauble and one for myself too. Gaudiness be damned! After coffee, I'd return and buy more. To gather armfuls in front of her seemed crass somehow.

We continued to chat, at first about her daughter in Australia, Steffie, and how happy she was with her new life in the sun. I enquired whether the fires that had ravaged parts of the country earlier in the year had affected her. Thankfully not. Not immediately, anyway. She'd been far enough removed, though the skies had become strange. She then asked about me, and so I told her about the house, the project.

"Carfax House?" she repeated. "Never heard of it. Grand name, though. Is it very big?"

"Big enough," I said rather ruefully. "A project that'll take a lifetime, that's for sure."

"A legacy, then?"

"A legacy?"

"For your children? And your children's children."

"Oh yes, I see. Definitely. We're going to take our time doing it up, really think about how we want it to look. It's listed, so we can't change much, but we can at least make it special again."

"Lot of grand houses around these parts," she said, lifting her coffee to take a sip. "All fallen to wrack and ruin."

"I'm sure."

"How long's it stood empty for?"

"A long time. We bought it blind at auction."

"And now that you know what it's like, do you stand by your decision?"

Interesting question. Did I? Now that I knew what it amounted to. "We'll make it work," I said. "Where do you live?"

"Me?" Another burst of bright laughter. "Oh, just a modest two-up two-down in Coleshill. Been retired a long time, but neither me nor my husband could be called highflyers, not like you and your husband – a lawyer, you say he is, in London? Fancy! And you a journalist? No, Don worked in a factory, and I worked in a shop. We're simple folk, really."

"What does your daughter do?"

"Raises her children, mainly. But she also works part-time keeping books. Her husband installs air-conditioning. He's got his own business and earns good money at it. They've got such a lovely house." Having divulged that information, she reached across the table and took my hand in hers. "Your husband will be home for Christmas, won't he?"

"Oh yes!" I assured her. "He's coming up tomorrow, by train."

"That's good. And the trains are running okay, are they?"

"Last time I checked." Which, in all honesty, I hadn't. I'd just presumed.

"Don't want you to be on your own for Christmas."

"You will be, though," I pointed out.

"I'm an old lady. It doesn't matter about me, not anymore. I'm used to it."

Immediately I protested. "It does matter! It…it always matters. Look, this has been lovely, meeting you, chatting with you."

"It has, dear. I've enjoyed it thoroughly."

"Do you have a mobile or a landline? It'd be nice to keep in touch. Meet again. If you wanted to, that is."

"Really?" How surprised she looked!

"Oh, no pressure. It was just a thought."

"My dear," she said, she *insisted*, "I'd like to, I really would. I'm surprised that you want to, that's all."

A grin spread across my face. I hoped it wasn't a foolish grin, but inside I felt exactly that, foolishly happy. "You're the first person I've met up here, and…that's kind of special."

"It is, dear, it is. I have a mobile, all the mod cons," she said, chuckling. Reaching into her handbag, where she'd also placed the carefully wrapped bauble I'd bought her earlier, she retrieved her phone, tapping away at its screen. "Just got to look my number up," she explained, her expression one of concentration. "Can never remember the darned thing. Got a proper phone too, so I'll also give you that. Best to have them both."

Having saved both numbers on my mobile, I sent her a text with my details.

Our coffees were finished.

We made our way outside to find no more blue skies but drizzle.

"Blast," Patricia said, "I've forgotten my brolly."

"Oh, I've got one," I said, reaching into my bag now to search for a navy-blue telescopic that I kept handy. "Take this."

"No, no," she protested. "I couldn't possibly."

"Not gonna argue about it," I replied. "Don't want you getting wet."

"You are very kind, dear," she said.

"And as I've said before, you're most welcome."

Her hands closed around it, again our fingers brushing, such close contact, such…warmth.

"Well, then," she said, opening the umbrella and holding it aloft so that we could both stand beneath it, "we will definitely have to meet so I can return this."

"I'll call you."

I turned to go, but her next words stopped me in my tracks.

"I don't normally do what I did today," she said.

I turned back. "Sorry, I'm not sure I understand. Do what?"

"Talk to strangers," she explained before a brief burst of hearty laughter. "You spend so long telling your children not to do it and then go and do it yourself!"

I inclined my head, curious. "So, why did you?"

She shrugged. "Who knows? But I'm glad I did. Make sure Al gets home for Christmas, okay? Make sure you have yourselves a merry old time. You deserve it."

"We all do." My voice was a whisper as I walked away.

* * *

After meeting Patricia, I ventured into further stores, maxing out credit cards that had already suffered enough. I bought a new tree – a real one, not the plastic one we'd had in London and brought to Carfax House – and dragged it to my nearby car, glad I'd got a Sorento, that its boot was huge once you'd pushed the back seats down. We'd been lucky enough to have a parking space in London; not that we'd ever used the car there, only for jaunts out of town, but it would certainly come in handy now, utilised for mad shopping sprees such as this one. Tinsel, paper decorations and an inflatable snowman were also purchased, and baubles, of course. I got fresh holly too, to decorate the bannister even though there were probably a dozen holly trees in the garden yet to be discovered.

Last stop was Marks and Spencer, and then I'd return home, a small glow inside me – just a spark, but I hoped it would keep alight, that it would grow.

Christmas, I'm coming atcha!

In the car, I switched to a Christmas channel on the radio, a little tired of the songs but not yet willing to admit it. It was only for a few more days, and then they'd vanish like smoke into the ether, not to be played again for another eleven months.

The drizzle had continued whilst I was shopping, but on the drive back to Carfax House, it stopped, the skies pale with no blue at all.

Country roads, single lane. Not overly busy, which I was glad about.

My eyes strayed every so often from the road to what lay around me. In spring, trees would be bounteous instead of bare, and fields that special green, which was fresh and crisp with hints of yellow in it. It would be beautiful, not that it wasn't now; to say so would be incorrect. But it was…a bleak beauty, a beauty that was…heartbroken.

I shook this thought from my head, pushing it aside as another jolly song came on, the Spice Girls with their festive hit 'Christmas Wrapping'. I sang along. I'd have some Christmas wrapping of my own to do soon. Besides a new tree and plenty of decorations, I'd bought Al a gift, a watch, one I knew he'd had his eye on. Al loved watches. Just like shoes and handbags are some women's thing, although not mine, watches were his. Yes, it had been expensive – I'd had to dip further into savings to buy it, savings that were much needed – but I didn't see it as just a Christmas present, rather, something to mark the occasion. His arrival. Being reunited. Life starting anew.

The house wasn't far now, set in deep countryside, the memory of Birmingham's busy city centre already feeling dreamlike. Even the meeting with Patricia Brown felt that way. Had I really offered to buy her a bauble? A stranger, as she'd described me. It was a nice gesture, admitted, but not one I'd ever succumbed to before. In London you lived cheek by jowl with so many people, yet rarely did you make eye contact, let alone buy them something! I was glad I'd done it, though, that I'd made a friend. I liked Patricia; she was sweet. She was brave too, a woman whose family were a million miles away, or might as well be, but who kept on smiling, kept on being cheerful.

Almost there. There were no villages hereabouts. The last one, Durston, was several miles back and appeared to be just a cluster of houses. At Carfax House, we really were out in the boondocks. It was a wonder we even got 4G.

The sky was white, and the mist was too. It was rising. Again.

I glanced at the clock on the dash. It was nearing four o'clock. The sun was already low in the sky. Soon, there'd be darkness once more, and isolation.

I almost sailed right past the turnoff, which would have been a pain as there was no convenient place close by to perform a U-turn. Just…a road that stretched on and on.

Thankfully, there was no one behind me when I slammed on the brakes. Reversing a fraction, I turned into the road that would lead to the driveway of a house that had once been grand but since abandoned – until we came along.

And saved it.

"Whoa! Don't get ahead of yourself. You haven't saved anything yet!"

But we will. We will.

I parked up, aware that I'd kept my eyes lowered on the approach to the house, had only barely lifted them. Outside the car, I hurried to the boot, anxious to unpack. Grabbing some bags first, I proceeded on, eyes still lowered, but I had to raise them eventually. There it was. Carfax House. Misty tendrils began to unfurl in the branches of naked trees, leisurely making their way towards it. It was winter. Deep winter. Of course the house looked forbidding. But it wouldn't always. That's what I had to focus on. In time, this would be a refuge, a sanctuary, a place to run to, not from.

Although someone had, a long time ago. And no one had wanted it since.

Once I'd unpacked everything and was inside, I'd be what…trapped?

No. Not at all. This was home. *Home!* I'd agreed to this. I'd wanted this.

We'll save you. More than that, we'd love the house. We'd be passionate about it.

The carrier bags I held in my hands were the first step in that process.

Carfax House, you're going to be amazing!

Chapter Eight

Christmas. Such a wonderful time. But I was also glad it came but once a year. Decorating a house like this was proving exhausting! Plus, the Christmas songs really were beginning to grate. Still, not long and it'd be a new year in every sense, a year that would see a lot of hard work being done, both professionally and in transforming this house.

So, I continued to sing along. I smiled. And I considered going outside to find logs and twigs to make a fire in what would be the main living room but decided not to. Rushing around, climbing up and down a stepladder to hang decorations meant I was warm enough.

Chris Rea's 'Driving Home for Christmas' came on again, my favourite song of the bunch, I decided, because the sentiment put me in mind of Al and the journey he'd soon be on. As Rea said, it was going to take some time, but he'd get home eventually, and so would Al. I couldn't wait to see his face when he stood outside Carfax House for the first time. Lights would be blazing and the Christmas tree twinkling in the window. When he stepped inside, I'd have the radio on, not a Christmas channel but one that was lively enough, and a meal on the go that emitted smells to make your mouth water.

A different homecoming to mine, one that would make his dark eyes shine.

"Happy Christmas," I'd say, wrapping my arms around him. And we'd stand there in the entrance hall, that spark of excitement becoming a furnace.

Standing in front of the tree now, breathing in its rich, piney scent, I reached for another decoration to hang from its many layered branches. I hadn't gone with a theme – some years I did, some years I didn't – I'd just bought whatever had taken my fancy. I was placing upon it a ballerina in a frosted pink tutu, caught forever in a pirouette. Such a pretty piece, she could occupy a central position, with baubles and other trinkets on either side of her. It was the sort of decoration a little girl would love...the little girl in me...

"It looks beautiful, darling. Really nice. Well done. You're making such an effort."

It was my mother's voice I was recalling, a memory from long ago, although I knew exactly how old I was: eight.

I'd been decorating the tree in another living room in another house. Not a tree in any way as grand as this, a small tree, artificial, but weren't they mostly artificial back then?

The TV had been on, a game show or something equally banal, and we had the volume right down. Force of habit, I suppose.

It had been a few days before Christmas, maybe even Christmas Eve-Eve, as I used to call it when I was younger than eight, the day before the twenty-fourth. There was a time when we'd put the tree up way in advance, but not anymore.

Just a tree. A small tree. But it was something. A gesture.

It hadn't taken me long to finish it, and then I'd stood back to admire it.

Pretty. Festive. White lights glittering.

And tears sprang to my eyes.

Mum had left the room by then; she'd gone back into the kitchen to make dinner. I was glad I was alone. The last thing I wanted was for her to see me crying.

A sound other than the TV reached my ears. For a moment I stood there confused, and then I realised what it was. Carol singers!

They'd knocked on the door and burst into song.

Tearing my gaze from the tree, I headed out of the living room and into the hallway.

"Mum," I shouted. "There are carol singers at the door!"

"Are there?" I heard her say before she turned from the stove and entered the hallway too.

Her red-rimmed eyes glistened in the hallway light. Briefly they flickered upwards to the floor above before settling on the door again.

"So there are," she continued, her voice little more than a whisper.

What was it with the Christmas carols? Some of them were so melancholic, and this one was no exception.

In the bleak midwinter,
Frosty wind made moan,
Earth stood hard as iron
Water like a stone…

Whoever was singing – they sounded mainly female – were glorious, though. Voices high, sweet and harmonious. The sound permeated the house, travelling down the hallway towards us, where we were still standing as if transfixed, rooted to the spot. Tears fell from Mum's eyes, and they fell from mine too. What was the point in hiding them?

"Mum" – my voice had become a whisper too – "what shall we do?"

The answer, when it came, was as desolate as the song.

"I don't know," she replied. "I have no idea what we're going to do."

* * *

I needed a drink. Badly.

The ballerina dangling, I padded out of the living room in slippered feet, along the corridor and back to the kitchen, barely glancing at the stairwell as I went, keeping my eyes straight ahead.

We'd already had the Belling cooker in the kitchen, and now, courtesy of the removal men, we had a fridge, albeit one barely fit for purpose just like the dining table, that had suited our small kitchen but not a vast space like this. It worked, though, and would do until we could head to the shops in the January sales and get one of those American fridge-freezers complete with an ice dispenser that Al had been drooling over.

I'd crammed as much food as possible into the fridge, and white wine too. What I couldn't get in I'd placed in the scullery by the back door. It was so cold in there any food was bound to be okay. Red wine was in the cupboard, so it wouldn't become too chill.

It was a bottle of white I wanted, grabbing a glass and

filling it to the brim. I gulped it straight down, half of me horrified at how fast I was drinking, issuing a silent reprimand, the other half metaphorically sticking two fingers up, not giving a damn.

The minute I finished the glass, I refilled it, but this time I forced myself to sip more slowly. My hand was shaking, and, subsequently, the wine was sloshing about. My other hand was busy raking through my hair.

I wished Al were with me. With all my heart I wished that.

And Mum…I wished she were too. That memory of us standing in the hallway with the carol singers insisting on finishing 'In the Bleak Midwinter' hadn't surfaced for a long time.

Mum was long gone, however. She'd died when I was in my mid-twenties. Cancer. I couldn't help but think there'd been another reason, though, one that couldn't be scientifically proven. A *silent* reason. Through it all, Al had been my rock. And then we'd got married. Although not something that was particularly important to Al, he knew it meant a lot to me. He'd just wanted me to be happy.

And I was happy on our wedding day.

In the photos, which were upstairs in a box that hadn't yet been opened, you could see how much I was smiling. There wasn't one photograph in which I wasn't.

Mum would have loved to have been there, because that's all she'd wanted, some happiness too.

The lights flickering overhead interrupted my thoughts.

I tilted my head. *What the hell?*

They flickered, then tripped out, but only for a second or two before coming back on.

The radio had also stopped, but for some reason didn't return with the lights.

My phone was on the table, so I picked it up. In terms of 4G, it had flatlined.

Just a glitch, that's all. And a possible explanation for why the radio had cut out the previous night. Hopefully, normality would resume soon, as I wanted to phone Al tonight, check what train he'd be on tomorrow, what time I'd need to pick him up from the station. A glitch, nothing more. It was to be expected that reception would falter out here. And the weather didn't help. I looked towards the window, at the mist, the shield wall.

Everything was so quiet, the atmosphere…reverential.

I'd gulped my wine before, and I did so again, knocked the second glass back. Heading for the radio, I picked it up and shook it. It yielded a bit of static but nothing more, a hissing that made me shudder, reminding me of the wall sconce and how that had hissed.

"Bloody thing," I muttered, this precious Roberts radio of mine.

What should I do now? There was no radio and no TV. I wasn't particularly hungry; the wine had seen to that. And it was dark outside, and misty.

Finish the decorating.

But there was little more to do. The downstairs was finished. The upstairs…could wait.

Admire what you've done, then.

Yes, I could, I supposed. All that hard work.

I hadn't bothered decorating the kitchen or the study, just the entrance hall, what would become the main living room, the corridors and the stairwell.

I thought I'd bought enough to do more rooms, but, clearly, I'd miscalculated.

Depending on what time Al arrived, I could do more shopping in the morning, see to the other rooms. But would a paper chain or a bit of tinsel really make much difference?

In the entrance hall, it *had* made a difference. It was pretty, so much cheerier than before. Huge white snowflakes hung from the ceiling, several of them, and stars too, some of them golden and glittering and twirling this way and that. I'd also trailed tinsel and paper chains widthways rather than lengthways – the length of the hall was just too long – a riot of colour when, before, it had been so plain.

Beside the door, in pride of place, stood the inflatable snowman, boasting black eyes and a carrot for a nose. Around its neck I'd tied an old scarf of mine, a chequered one. The whole place looked cute. It looked fun, like a child had been let loose, filled to overflowing with enthusiasm. Funny how the adult version of that child didn't feel that way now and was nowhere near as enthusiastic but, instead, biting at her lip and wondering if she should have gone more classic in style. *So hard on yourself.* That's what Al sometimes said to me. He meant in terms of my work; I was never quite happy with a piece, always trying to tweak it right up until the deadline. *A perfectionist.* Maybe.

Was that a tear on my cheek?

I reached up to find that, sure enough, it was.

Surprised, I rubbed at it, making it disappear.

The living room – I'd go in there and gaze at the tree instead.

There it was, standing in a cold and empty room, no fire in the grate, although there would be tomorrow. The mist at the window seemed to be peering at it too, just as I was.

No doubt about it, it was a thing of beauty. Its fresh scent not quite enough to overcome the smell of damp but having an impact, at least. It was impressive. Like the house was. And yet there was no one to admire it. Just me. No Al, no mother and no friends.

Of course, we would invite friends, and we would invite Al's parents, separately, on account they didn't get on. And they'd all come, they'd be happy to. Curious. Although…I had to admit, I had no close friends. I had…acquaintances. Those I went out with once the working day was done, fellow journalists and writers that had come together to form a community. There was Deborah, Linda, Ray, Eddie, Sarah and Joe. People with whom I'd drink too much at various pubs, chew the cud with over dinner regarding certain issues. We'd have some raging debates over environmentalism and feminism. Friends who, when I'd told them about our project, had widened their eyes in awe.

"Seriously, you're leaving London?"

That was mainly the response. As if only lunatics would entertain such an idea. Leaving not just hustle and bustle but the centre of the universe.

To isolate myself.

Friends, acquaintances, were they the same thing or something entirely different to each other? In leaving London, had I severed the link that connected us? Was I just part of a circle and therefore easily replaced, leaving a space that the next person could step into, as though it were some kind of ritual, some kind of dance? Although curious, would they really visit, or would they blame busy schedules as an excuse not to? No close friends. No…best friend. No one to pour my heart out to, whom I could get on the phone to when my signal returned and say, "Tell me honestly, have we done the right thing with this house move? It's over an hour from London, right? It's not that big a deal."

How amazing to hear a voice, reassuring me that, no, it wasn't a big deal, not at all.

Not Al's voice, someone else's.

Sarah's, even, whom, out of the group, I perhaps got on best with, who would whisper to me on so many occasions, "Let's split, leave this lot to it, go grab something to eat."

A woman who'd wanted to get to know me better, and yet…

"Sure," I'd say, "but it's my round. Soon after, though?"

'Soon after' never came. Once I'd got the drinks in, it'd then be someone else's round and me the first to say, "Oh, go on, then, I'll have another vino." I'd catch her looking at me, and I'd shrug. And she would smile and shrug too. Might as well stay.

"We could go shopping." She'd also suggested that. "Stock up on power suits," she'd add with a smile.

"Al and I are busy this weekend," I'd answer. "We're going to visit his mother. She lives in the West Country, pig of a drive, terrible traffic on a Friday, but it'll be nice to see her. Another time, though. God knows I could do with some new jeans. Mine are getting tight!"

But just as tomorrow never came, neither did 'another time'.

I wondered now. Why not?

She'd tried to get closer, but she gave up.

Because, ultimately, she was busy too? Or because I'd just kept on pushing her away?

And I'd pushed her away because…it was easier?

I'd never questioned this before, never really had the time to.

But now, in this big old mausoleum of a house, this sow's ear despite the sparkles, there seemed to be nothing but time. Nothing but silence too.

Was Patricia Brown, a woman I didn't even know, the closest thing I had to a friend?

From the living room, I reentered the entrance hall, with the staircase in front of me, holly bound to its bannister with ribbon, green leaves and red berries trying to make it more enticing. As I stared at it, the lights above flickered again, perhaps trying to keep time with the flashing lights on the Christmas tree, joining in.

Silence. And a hiss.

I almost threw myself forward, back towards the kitchen. There was virtually nothing left in the open bottle of white, so I'd open another. And another if needs be.

Bring this day to an end.

Chapter Nine

Was my mind playing tricks with me again? Was I hearing correctly?

Footsteps, pacing. Not stomping footsteps but light – and determined.

I'd positioned a lamp by my bed in the study, and I reached out a hand, fumbling for the switch, my head pounding and my throat as dry as parchment. With the room illuminated, I glanced at my watch. Like the first night when I'd awoken, it was just after three, a fact that made me frown. I'd drunk enough to sink a small battleship earlier; by rights, I should still be out for the count. But I wasn't. I was wide awake, sitting up and listening.

Were they footsteps?

Was it possible I was still asleep and this a dream?

There was no one upstairs.

There shouldn't be.

There was only me. Holed up, incarcerated, buried alive.

STOP!

God, what was wrong with me? Why did such thoughts crowd my mind? Horrible thoughts, unwelcome, that had no place in my life, thoughts that I wouldn't entertain.

There was no one in this house besides me.

And yet those were footsteps I could hear. For certain. Too measured to belong to an animal that might have found its way in, like a rat. Too…deliberate.

Overhead. In one of the bedrooms.

I did the calculation. It'd be the bedroom opposite the one I'd chosen, to the right of it if you were standing facing the house.

I should go and see.

As I began to shuffle forwards, swinging my legs onto the floor, I also registered how cold it was and that the radio was off. Either I hadn't bothered or been too drunk to turn it back on. To be honest, I barely remembered going to bed. I hadn't undressed; I still had my jeans and jumper on.

What was that film where the mist had enclosed the house? *The Others,* that was it, starring Nicole Kidman, one of my favourite actresses. And the mist had done so for a reason. *But not the same reason,* I told myself, growing so cross with my active imagination. But I was a writer, a reader, I loved films. Could I really expect anything less?

Go and investigate.

I didn't want to. There, I'd admitted it. Just like I hadn't wanted to the last time. Indeed, I hadn't been back upstairs, since…since…

Taking a deep breath, I exhaled.

My body was shaking again. My hands were.

This is my house!

Yet, admittedly, it was new to me; it was alien, a house bigger than any I'd ever lived in before, that you could fit several of my childhood house into, and many more than that of the London flat. Not counting various uni digs and equally scruffy rentals, it was my third ever residence. A grand house that had been left to decay.

What if it's haunted?

"SHIT!"

I screamed so loud I startled myself. Had I startled what was above me too? Stopped them in their tracks?

Back and forth. Back and forth.

Someone was up there. Not a ghost, surely? A ghost would glide, wouldn't it?

Just go and fucking see.

I stood up, the room swaying as much as me.

Was I still drunk? I had to be. Alcohol took time to leave your system; it didn't dissipate just like that. I frowned as I tried to remember how much I'd drunk, a memory of not just one bottle but two, three, even.

Bloody hell, the cold was biting. I reached for my dressing gown, shrugged it on over my clothes and tied it tight. It didn't make a blind bit of difference. I'd turned all the electric heaters in the house to max. I'd done that a while ago, and during the day it was okay, it was bearable, doors to rooms kept shut, especially those whose windows were cracked. By night, though, when temperatures naturally dipped, it could be arctic.

Had the noise stopped, or had I simply grown used to it? Was there an accompanying, echoing whisper? No. Just the pacing. All was silent otherwise. I swallowed, tried to calm breathing that was growing rapid. This was my house, and I refused to be frightened in it. Leaving my room, I headed towards the kitchen first. No way would I go up there unprepared. I opened a drawer and grabbed a knife, the meanest-looking one, used for chopping meat. I'd hurt no one before, and I didn't want to now. Perhaps I couldn't.

Faced with an intruder, I'd probably drop the knife and run. I'd find out soon enough.

Before I left the kitchen, my eyes strayed over to the sink to the empty bottles there. There were three of them, although the third still had some wine in it. My jaw dropped open. Had I ever drunk that much before? When out with friends, perhaps, over the course of an evening, but not on my own. I couldn't beat myself up about it, though. There were other, more urgent matters to attend to.

As I started back down the corridor, I realised something: it *was* the drink that was emboldening me. The sensible thing to do was to grab my mobile phone and my car keys, quietly let myself out, head to the car and get out of here, call the police, let them investigate instead. I could just imagine what they'd say in response:

"Carfax House? Where's that? Never heard of it."

And what I would say in reply:

"That's because it's a lonely house, it's a forgotten house. A house that even vandals and teenagers looking for the next thrill have left well alone."

"Where is it, then?"

"It's on the road past the village of Durston, about twelve or thirteen miles on from it, travelling west. Closer by is a farm, Frogmore, but even that's around four miles away. The lane I'm down is Bonnington Lane, and about three-quarters of the way up is a right turn. Take that right turn and keep going. That's where I am. Where you'll find me."

Alone. But equipped.

And determined.

This had to be dealt with. Now.

This was a dream house, or it would be. Not the stuff of

nightmares.

I could have shouted as I walked, I could have issued a warning, but that would only serve to alert whomever it was. They could then flee and hide. The person that was pacing had to be the same one responsible for those echoing whispers I'd heard. If so, where did they hide during the day? Where did they go?

Creeping in the dark, that's what I was doing, like a spider, scuttling along. One hand on the wall, feeling my way. Wondering at such darkness and how expansive everything seemed within it, without boundary, but also knowing that was nonsense. I'd worked out by now how many steps to take and where, the layout becoming less of a mystery.

At the stairs, I hesitated.

Get in the car and drive.

I was too drunk to drive.

Doesn't matter. Not out here. Needs must. Go on, go. You're mad if you don't.

Mad? No. I wasn't.

It's dark up there.

So dark. But there was darkness at my back too.

You could get hurt.

Or I could solve this once and for all.

My foot was on the bottom stair, but again I hesitated.

Do you really want to know?

"This is my house," I whispered. That was my sole argument, my only reason for putting myself in jeopardy. We'd sold the London flat, and, yes, we could buy another, but only if we sold this first. Yet who would want it? What other fools?

I shook my head, an attempt to thwart any more rogue thoughts.

Keep climbing. And don't touch the bannister; holly could be vicious, like barbed wire.

On the landing, I stopped. No moonlight filtered in through the windows, only mist, but it diluted the gloom a fraction, at least. I had to turn right, towards the source of the pacing, although my gaze was drawn left, to the sixth bedroom and what lay beyond the ancient oak door within. Silence. Only silence from there. No whisper at all and no hissing lights.

Turning right, the closer I got to the sound of the pacing, the fainter it became, as if intent on teasing me. I had to hurry, remember where the light switch was in that bedroom, reach for it as I hurled myself in there, my other hand holding the knife, a fierce look on my face. *Who are you? What do you want? THIS IS MY HOUSE!*

I ran down that corridor, feet pounding on the floorboards, did as I intended and entered the room in a fury, one hand reaching out, the bare light bulb dutifully bursting into life.

There was nothing. There was no one.

I think I knew all along there wouldn't be.

There was just me standing there, brandishing a weapon, my dressing gown having come undone, my eyes scanning from side to side.

It was empty.

Completely.

Just like me.

Chapter Ten

No, this wasn't right, this was too much.

I couldn't believe what I was hearing.

"Tell me you're not serious."

"Look, Lizzie, I'm sorry. Really sorry. But the partners are taking me out for lunch, only me, not the rest of the firm. A jolly's been arranged for the others elsewhere. Liz, did you hear what I said? This lunch thing, it's going to be *just* me. You know what that means, don't you? They're gonna pop the question about a partnership. It's everything we've worked towards, that we've dreamed of. Shit, Liz, can you believe it?"

"But you promised…" I said, my voice drifting away. "You'd be here today."

"Liz, this is all last-minute. Literally, they've just sprung it on me. But I'll be there tomorrow. Christmas Eve. The firm closes today, all work's been done. It's just this to sort now, the lunch, which – you know what these things are like – will likely go on and on, right into the evening. I could postpone it, could ask them if we could do it in the new year instead, but you know what? I don't think I could live with the suspense! I'd be like a cat on hot coals. I'm sorry, so sorry, but give me tonight, and then in the morning, I'm outta here, leaving the rat race behind. The whole of Christmas will be ours to enjoy."

"And then what?"

The pleading in Al's voice gave way to confusion. "What do you mean, then what?"

"Will you really commute to London from here, or will you grow tired of it and just stay put in London, hole up in another hotel, come home at weekends, if that?"

"What? I'll commute! No problem. Yeah, sure, I'll have to stay over in London sometimes, but we've discussed all this, you know all this. You'll have to come and stay too every now and then, not just because of work but to catch up with friends, to network, to…you know…get your London fix. This will work out, it will. Liz? Talk to me. I can hear you breathing, so I know you haven't cut me off. You're still there."

"It's fine."

"What's that? What did you say?"

"I said it's fine. Go ahead. Have lunch, dinner, whatever, and…I hope it's good news."

"It is. It will be. This is us set for life, Lizzie. This is us made."

"Yeah, yeah, it's great."

"Happy bloody Christmas, eh?"

I laughed. "Absolutely."

There was another silence. "Liz, you okay?"

"I'm fine. Drank a bit too much last night, got a sore head."

"Really? On your own?"

"It was good wine."

He laughed this time. "And you still love the house?"

Still love it? "It'll be great."

"I really am sorry about this."

"It can't be helped."

"Tomorrow I'm there, come hell or high water."

"I know. I know."

"Speak to you later, okay? As soon as I can, I'll call you."

"I'll keep my phone handy."

"I did try and call you last night, actually, but there was no reply."

"The signal can dip."

"Plus, you were tipsy."

"Yeah."

"Speak to you later, then. More cleaning today, unpacking?"

"Yep, there's still loads to do."

"Can't wait to see. To see you too."

"Me too. Speak later. Love you."

It was another conversation done. My husband had been reduced to a voice on the end of the phone. Not someone to have and to hold, to be held by.

Shit, what have we done!

I took several deep breaths. It would be fine. All of it. Life was only going to get better. Why the heck was I letting a big house freak me out like this? People lived in big houses, plenty of them. They took on renovation projects. I wasn't the first and wouldn't be the last. And big houses could be quirky. There was room for quirkiness, for…unusual features.

I placed my phone on the kitchen table on charge; the battery clearly needed replacing, as it kept running low. I'd spend some time this morning baking biscuits, and then

I'd…do what? Go gather some wood from the garden, not put it off any longer, try and get a fire going. That would cheer me. I could sit in front of it, imagining myself on an old Chesterfield sofa rather than the grey Ikea one we had, Victorian lamps gracing each corner.

An hour later and the smells in the kitchen were heady, cinnamon and other spices better than any scented candle. I used to love baking biscuits as a kid. Funny how I'd only ever done it at Christmastime, decorating them either in white or lurid colours.

When had been the last time I'd done this? Just a kid, nine, ten, or maybe eleven. I'd baked them and brought them to the table for my mother to admire. And she *had* admired them. She'd lifted her head and smiled at me.

"They're lovely."

But she hadn't taken one; she'd just looked at them.

I don't think I tried one either.

But these I would.

Retrieving them from the oven, I had to admit, they looked pretty good. Golden in the middle, slightly darker and crispier around the edges. I'd used a cookie cutter. Some were in the shape of trees and some like snowmen disguised as Mr Blobby! Encapsulating Christmas in biscuit form. I smiled, almost forgot about the headache I had.

Forgot something else too, to turn the radio on. This morning it just…hadn't crossed my mind. Maybe I was getting used to the silence. Or I was listening out.

But there was nothing, no noise at all.

The reason, perhaps, why my thoughts were getting louder.

I'd switch on the radio, but not before I headed outside

to get that firewood.

It was cold, and a residue of mist remained, hovering above the ground here and there. Wrapped up warm enough, I skirted around the tangle of bushes and hedges, having to duck sometimes beneath low branches. This was the furthest I'd been in, what…three days? A short time, really, although it seemed much longer than that, like…years.

A rustle in the bushes captured my attention. A blur of grey, something that quickly disappeared. A rabbit? This garden would be teeming with life, most of it unseen. Just a blur of rabbit and – I tipped my head backwards – a bird here or there, swooping low. Not today, though; there were either no birds in the sky or the low-hanging clouds obscured them. Perhaps the clouds were soaking up sound too, as it was as quiet out here as it was inside, only the sound of my breathing as I continued on.

I'd brought a bag with me, one of those supermarket bags for life, and now and then I'd stoop to pick up branches and bits of wood suitable for burning. I was enjoying myself, I realised, the exercise. Back in London I was a member of a gym, but I'd hardly ever visited. I had walked, though, loads, easily meeting my daily target of ten thousand steps, kept trim that way. I didn't think I'd cancelled that gym membership; I'd forgotten about it. I'd make a note, get around to it.

I continued foraging, my bag getting heavier and heavier. Shopping of a different kind. My mind returned to Patricia. Should I text her? See how she was? Suggest meeting up for a coffee again in the town centre once Christmas was over. I'd send Sarah a text too. I could phone, but a text first, to each of them. Make the effort.

There was another rustle. Another rabbit? I turned, saw nothing, walked forward, then tripped.

"Ow!"

Tumbling down, I fell half onto the bag of wood and half onto something else. Something hard. Stone? Could it be?

It *was* stone. Hard and unyielding. Scrambling to my feet, I took a step back and then another. Earlier, whilst on the phone to Al, I couldn't believe what I was hearing, and now I couldn't believe what I was seeing. A grave. Right there, in the grounds of Carfax House. It was so overgrown that roots had risen up and were clinging to it, as if intent on claiming the stone for the soil and the body beneath.

The house had been built in 1868, one hundred and fifty-two years ago, so this was an old grave. It had to be.

At the head of it was a cross, a small one, and that, too, was covered in roots as bleached as the sky. Having stifled my shock, I drew closer to it and hunkered down. There was no carving on the cross; rather, it was plain. Instead, the stone border surrounding the grave was carved and so deeply covered with moss and lichen that it was difficult to read. I reached out and tried to scrape away some of the moss with my hands in order to read the epitaph. It was no use, for the letters seemed to have weathered. A forgotten house and a forgotten grave. Were there more graves to be stumbled upon? Parents, brothers, sisters of this person, or other family members?

I stood up, scanning the landscape all around me. I couldn't find evidence of others. Just this one, then. Not a fancy grave but not one where someone had skimped either. Why had they been buried here? Was it a request? Maybe, once upon a time, this house had been so loved that this person couldn't bear to leave it. Not even in death.

The sound of a crow in the trees startled me.

So, there were birds here. They hadn't forsaken the place.

What the hell? *Why would they forsake it? It's a house, just a house. Go back inside.*

I'd do that, gather the wood I'd dropped and head to the study, where my laptop was, hoping the 4G was going strong, that I could hotspot from my phone.

* * *

Sold unseen. No visit beforehand, no time, as we were too busy and too worried the house would suddenly be snapped up – that if we dithered, we'd lose it, our desire for it somehow creating a chain reaction. It'd been a case of get our flat on the market, get the bid in and wing it, basically. Seal the deal. And we had. We'd been successful. We'd bought ourselves a house we knew nothing about, other than it needed repair. A home that, at some point in the future, would offer 'ideal family living', the estate agents' words, not ours. It all seemed so irrational now in hindsight.

We'd tried to look up a bit about it on the net beforehand, but we couldn't find much. In retrospect, I had to admit we hadn't tried *that* hard. The past was the past; that had been our reasoning. It was the future that had concerned us. Now, though, I needed to go further.

I read online that the best place to research the history of a house, its occupants and the surrounding area was in a local county archive. It was the twenty-third of December, in the afternoon, and therefore unlikely I'd make it to an archive hereabouts before closing time, even if I knew where one was. Tomorrow was Christmas Eve. Record offices would likely be shut. I had nothing but the internet to rely on, and that kept dipping in and out. Census records were available, taken between 1841 and 1911. I could make a start on them, but it wouldn't yield instant results; it'd be labour intensive. Another option was to fill out a form and request the title deeds, see what I could glean from them. Again, not an instant fix.

What about Simon Lilley, a renowned architect once upon a time? Was there anything about him online? I typed in his name, and various Simon Lilleys came up on screen. They were living people, though, an artist, a photographer, a Simon Lilley who worked for the UN Environment Programme, and an antiques dealer. None of them had lived in the nineteenth century and built Victorian residences.

The next obvious contender to type in the search bar was Carfax House itself. Yes, Al and I had done this, but no harm in repeating it.

I got one hit, that was it. And that was the auction details we'd already seen.

There was no more information. The trail had gone cold.

I sighed, got up and headed over to the kettle, intending to make myself a coffee.

Discovering that grave, it had…unsettled me further. There was a need in me, an ache to find out whom it belonged to. Overgrown and forgotten, it couldn't stay that way. I'd tend to it, clear the weeds. I could also try again to trace the carvings upon it with my fingertips, press really hard. Census records would give me a bunch of names but not *the* name.

The last owner of Carfax House had been a man named Thomas Lint. Aside from his name, I knew he'd inherited the house from another family member, but he'd never really lived here. Never sold it either, until now.

"Why not?" I remembered asking.

"No idea," the estate agent had replied. "Some people, though, they're loaded, aren't they? Enough to carry a property like this. To not give it a second thought."

"But they're selling it now," I'd reminded him.

"Yeah, they are. Money runs out. Eventually."

That was it, the only explanation I'd been given.

Although a listed building, that wouldn't necessarily stop any owner from letting it fall into ruin. Returning to my computer, coffee cup in hand, I resumed surfing the net and found out that the council could serve a listed building repairs notice, but if the owner said he or she had no money to do the work, there wasn't a lot they could do to enforce it. The only other option available would be for them to compulsorily purchase the house and do something with it. Again, it wasn't ever going to happen, as most councils struggled to fund essential 'statutory' services, let alone desirable but nonessential services.

And so, the house had deteriorated in someone else's possession, lived in occasionally, maybe, as a summer residence or party pad until, as the estate agent had said, they'd offloaded it. Cashed in, got what they could, cast adrift the weight of an inheritance.

And, clearly, it had been a weight. Because summer residence, party pad or not, it hadn't been loved, hadn't been cared for or nurtured. Lint hadn't been inspired by it.

The seller had wanted the estate agent to deal with all matters. And they had, perfectly well. The solicitors too. And never, not once, had there been mention of a grave on-site.

If a violent death had occurred at the property, recent law required the owners to disclose it, along with a whole host of other concerns. Suicide was another issue that might 'affect the enjoyment of the property or decrease its value'. There'd been no mention of that either. But what if something *had* happened, and it had just been…forgotten? Or concealed. If there was a village nearby, I could head there and knock on doors, explain who I was, that I was seeking information about the project we'd bought, see if anyone knew anything about its history, anything at all. The local church, the local priest, but there was no village, only Durston, and that was twelve miles away.

I was trembling again. Should I phone Al and let him know the latest?

My hand reached for the phone, intending to do just that. But then I stopped. Lunch with his bosses would be well underway by now and the wine flowing. If they were discussing a partnership like he'd hoped, like he'd dreamed and wished for, then it seemed unfair to disturb him. This was his moment of glory. The culmination of so many years' hard work. To ring him, to mention the grave, would be churlish.

A grave.

On our land.

Part of our property.

Our responsibility.

A tear sprang to my eye. More than one, several broke rank to race down my cheeks. *Our responsibility.* That hit home.

Not thinking anymore, more intent on action, I stood up, grabbed my coat and headed back outdoors, straight to the grave, crunching over leaves that were brown and brittle.

Like before, I knelt and clawed at the roots that wanted to devour it, desperate to free it somehow, as if what really covered it were chains as thick as those Dickens had draped around Jacob Marley in *A Christmas Carol*.

Who were you in life? What was your name? What type of person were you? Like Marley, was he or she guilty of so many sins? Or was such a thought sacrilege?

Revealing some of the lettering, I traced my fingers along what indent remained, trying to read, to gain some knowledge. At that moment, ignorance seemed like such a vast ocean, one in which I was drowning.

Who are you?

J... Was that a *J* I'd just traced? Fixing it firmly in my mind, I moved to the next letter. *O.* Then the next. *S. E.* My heart began racing. Despite the cold, I felt as if I was sweating. *P.*

No. Not that. It couldn't be.

I recalled the steps I'd heard the previous night, the pacing.

H.

Joseph. It was Joseph.

But it wasn't, because right next to it was another letter.

I.

N.

A.

Josephina!

Thank God! Thank God it wasn't Joseph.

A woman. Her surname lost to me, as the roots that strangled the next word were just too stubborn to remove with bare hands.

It didn't matter.

I knew enough.

A woman was buried here. Josephina. On home ground.

For a reason.

I retrieved my hand, hugged myself instead and glanced to the west.

The day was fading so quickly.

And the mist was creeping back.

Chapter Eleven

A quick call from Al confirmed the wine had indeed been flowing.

"How's it going?" I asked. "Apart from the drinking?"

"In the right direction. They're gearing up to it, I know they are. Dale and Adrian," he continued, referring to two of the partners, "keep looking at each other and smiling. Keep beaming at me too. Right now they're talking about the need to expand and how well I contribute to the firm. It's like they're waiting to deliver the best present ever!"

"Well, it will be, won't it?" I said, thinking about the watch and how eager I was to present it to him, some of that eagerness vanishing. When it came to the prospects of a partnership, it was hardly going to compare. "Look, Al, I'm pleased for you. I really am. But be careful about how much you drink and how late you stay out."

"Oh, Lizzie—"

"I'm not trying to spoil this special time for you. I'm just reminding you that you've got a train to catch tomorrow and something else that's special too, our new house."

"Yeah, yeah, I know."

Yeah, yeah, I know. Was that all he could say? And delivered in a tone that was bored almost, as if…as if I was nagging him.

"Al—"

"Look, I can't stay on for long. They think I've just nipped to the loo."

"Al, seriously, take it easy. Remember to drink plenty of water too."

"Will you stop nagging?"

There, he'd said it. It was out in the open. And, yes, there was a hint of amusement in his voice, a hint of affection, but I couldn't help it – something inside me exploded to hear it.

"What the fuck, Al? How fucking dare you!"

"Liz?" Straightaway, uncertainty replaced amusement. "I was only joking—"

"And don't say that either, that you were only joking! A joke is supposed to be funny, and that wasn't. That was downright disrespectful!"

His swallow was so hard I could hear it. "You're right, I'm sorry, stupid drink. But I didn't mean it. You know I didn't."

"You know what, I don't know a damn thing. You're getting drunk with your bosses, but for all I know that could be a big fat lie. You could be out with a woman—"

"A woman?"

"YES! You could be having an affair, and that's why you're taking your own sweet time in coming up here."

"Now, hang on a minute, Liz—"

"No, you hang on. Excuse after excuse you've given me. I was supposed to be alone here two days at the most. But this is the fourth day, tomorrow will be the fifth—"

"I'll be there tomorrow!"

"It's always tomorrow with you!"

"There've been reasons. Good reasons."

"Perhaps you won't come back tomorrow either. You'll be so hungover you'll miss your train. And I'll be forced to spend Christmas here alone. It'll be a crap Christmas because Christmas always is. It's a farce. A sham. And I've tried so hard. So fucking hard!"

My voice was so high it was ricocheting, words I shouted flying straight back at me, ending on a sob that nearly choked me, that forced me into silence, just as Al was silent.

"Liz," he whispered eventually. "What's all this about? It's like… This isn't you. This isn't what you do."

Lose my temper? Get angry? He was right. I was mild-mannered Liz, easygoing Liz, Liz who'd do anything to keep her husband happy. I was the Liz he wanted me to be, that *I* wanted me to be. Not Liz the nag, Liz who was…unravelling.

"I'll come home now, cut the lunch short—"

"No!"

"What? Why? Liz, you're clearly—"

"I'm not clearly anything."

"Liz, please."

I tried to keep my voice steady. "Look, I'm a bit…stressed, that's all."

"Stressed? Why?"

"Just because…" *Josephina.* "Nothing." I bit my lip. "I got my period today." A lie. "I'm feeling emotional."

"Oh, I see."

I almost laughed at that, albeit wryly. To a man, a period could explain away so much. "You know what?" I said. "I just need to rest. I've got my period, and I've done a lot

92

of…um…weeding in the garden. I'm exhausted. Have fun. Grab that partnership with both hands as soon as it's offered. It's great news, it really is, and I'm so damned proud of you. I need to fill a hot-water bottle and have an early night. I'll be fine tomorrow. I will."

"Liz, I'm sorry about, you know, not being with you from the start."

"Not your fault. You wanted to postpone it, remember?"

"Well, yeah."

"It'll all be worth it in the end."

There was another pause. "You sure you're okay? It's just, they're gonna think I've climbed out the window or something if I don't go back soon."

"Go. Enjoy yourself."

"I'll call you later, you know, as soon as."

"Yeah, yeah, do that."

"I can't believe me having an affair even crossed your mind. You're the only girl for me and you know it. I love you, Liz."

"I love you too."

We ended the call. He loved me. But how could you truly love someone you didn't know? And he didn't know me. Worse still, I didn't know myself either, not anymore.

I looked towards the window.

Why are you buried there, Josephina?

She was both a reminder and a mockery.

Oh, now that Al was gone, the silence was as heavy as ever. I could mask it, shake that Roberts radio of mine into action, listen to more Christmas songs. Bake more biscuits too, something different this time, ones with pieces of crystallised ginger in, perhaps – I'm sure I had a jar

93

knocking about somewhere – or add a bit of cocoa powder instead. Al loved biscuits; he'd devour them in no time. I could drink more wine, although not as much as I had yesterday, or I could do what I'd told Al I was going to do and get an early night.

I could do all those things.

Or I could do something else.

Head upstairs.

To the chapel.

And pray.

Just like Josephina had prayed so long ago.

Chapter Twelve

So much was written and recorded, but, by the same token, some things were *never* written and *never* recorded. Entire chapters of lives. Great swathes of information. Details that got lost, just as this house was lost, as those that lived in it – me and someone else, Josephina, I was sure of it – were lost. It was her whisper I heard echoing through the house, her tread above me. My mind's eye could picture her pacing to and fro, a woman, a young woman, tormented by sorrow, wringing her hands and biting at her lip.

A woman buried here for a reason.

A reason I was beginning to suspect.

We knew next to nothing about this house, not yet, not whom it had sheltered over the years or the happiness or sadness of its occupants – the bursts of laughter, the torrents of tears, the confidences that had been exchanged, and the recriminations. Emotions both sacred and profane. But a house knows; a house *retains*. Walls encapsulating lives being lived, able to absorb it all, holding on to memories and replaying them.

At the bottom of the staircase, I lingered. Such a grand staircase. I remembered how I'd envisioned a grand lady sweeping down it, wearing a taffeta dress, how I would sweep down it too, a twenty-first-century version, my husband at the bottom, loving the lie.

Another tear in my eye, but I wiped it away, focused instead on the holly. It looked so beautiful bound with ribbon to the balustrade. A simple but effective decoration. Did it bring the house to life? No, it didn't. This was a dead house. Not an inheritance foisted upon us but one we willingly shouldered. Oh, it needed more than holly to make it breathe! More than stars and snowflakes hanging from the ceiling, tinsel, paper chains, and a tree adorned with twinkling lights. It needed me too, its owner. Otherwise, what would happen? Whether Al was made a partner or not, there'd still be plenty of occasions when he'd be required to stay in London, day after day, night after night, as a new case reached its finale. And sure, I could accompany him, work from a hotel room, catch up with acquaintances, eat, drink and be merry. But then this house would continue to stand empty.

Unable to heal.

I flinched at that.

Was that a continuation of my own thoughts or an echoing whisper from another?

The chapel was my destination. Just a small room behind an ancient oak door.

A quirk.

Her domain. Josephina's.

Her house. Once upon a time.

And now it was mine.

I climbed the stairs, no creak or groan from the treads as I went. This was a house where pipes never kicked or rattled, where floorboards never settled. It was silent. *As quiet as the grave.* And because it was, other noises could be heard. Those from beyond the grave. Restless.

At the top of the stairs, I switched the lights on. As usual, they flickered, they hissed at me.

I faltered again, contemplated rushing back downstairs to lock myself in my study for the evening and wait for morning to come and for Al to arrive. The radio loud all the while with cheerful voices singing. But something in me resisted. I had become restless too; this house had seen to that. *She* had seen to it.

Drawn to the window first, I gazed out at the mist. The grave was to the left of the property. Was something there other than cold stone? Did something drift in the mist? A figure only slightly more solid. Was she aimless or determined? Just like Cathy, coming ever closer. *Let me in!*

I turned to the right, to the bedroom where I'd heard pacing, *anguished* pacing. There it was, only very faint, but it would amplify. I was sure of it.

No need to unlatch a window. She was in already. Her energy drenched every brick of this building. She was the mortar, the glue that held it together. There'd been others after her, but how long had they stayed? With how plain everything was, the décor, no one had ever put their stamp on it, made it their own. They'd left it neutral. Left it to her.

She'd paced, she'd prayed, and she'd died.

The other bedroom, the one at the far end that I'd christened the sixth bedroom, was where I was heading. I had to go now, had to hurry. How quickly night had fallen!

Picking up pace, I drifted forwards as she might drift, past the flickering lights, my shadow on the wall beside me.

So many closed doors except this one, which stood ajar.

Inside the sixth bedroom, I crossed from one corner to the other, not bothering with the light this time – it was the darkness I had to face. My hand closing around the iron ring of the oak door, I registered once again how cold it was. A chapel. Who'd include a chapel in their own home? It was a quirk, but one that had been made desperate use of.

My hands still around that cold ring, I shoved at the door and entered a room that was colder still. Not a big space, it was small, secretive and hidden away. A holy room? There'd been prayers uttered here; I'd heard them. Had God heard too? Had He listened?

Such desperation!

Such melancholy.

Oh, it was hard to bear. It was hard to…remember.

This room, with its stone altar, a stone step for kneeling and a stone bench behind me, was a room I'd only recently discovered and had since tried to push from my mind.

Like the grave, I hadn't told Al about it.

And yet here it was; here it remained.

And finally, it had drawn me back.

The kitchen was the heart of any normal home, but not here at Carfax House. The chapel was the epicentre. Where a heart had bled dry. What else the house was comprised of didn't matter. Not the bedrooms, the living rooms, nor that grand old staircase with the wood panelling beside it. In this moment, it was all about the chapel. And me. And her.

But first there was me.

In a place for reflection, I backed up to the stone bench, my head falling forwards as I sat, my hands clutched together and brought up to rest below my chin.

* * *

A burst of laughter that bubbled in my chest. A mother who was baking, who'd tied an apron around me and let me bake alongside her. Both of us were covered in flour, my mother asking what I wanted Santa to bring me for Christmas. So much! Every child dreams of unwrapping presents on a snowy morning, and I'd been such a good girl. I'd tried so hard to obey my mother, getting dressed for school, brushing my teeth, working diligently in class, my hand shooting up to answer as many questions as I could, eating all my dinner, going to bed on time, not making a fuss and being quiet in the house, always quiet. Even now, whilst we were laughing, the radio on and playing cheerful tunes – but low, nothing more than a hum – we were quiet. Both of us stifling giggles as we pelted one another with flour, as we ran clean fingers around the rim of the bowl and licked at the cookie dough.

Be quiet. Always.

Or he'd get upset.

He couldn't bear noise.

It was shoes off at the door and tiptoe around. When talking, go into the kitchen to do it. The living room was directly beneath my parents' bedroom, otherwise, and he would hear us.

"Mum," I asked once, "why does he sleep so much?"

"Because he's tired," she'd answered.

I screwed up my nose. It didn't make sense. "All the time?"

"Yes, Lizzie, all the time."

But Christmas was coming. I was seven, and I'd looked

forward to it all year, even more so than my birthday, which was in August at the very height of summer.

I would tingle with anticipation, loving all the decorations that we made at school and the shops that bulged with toys, their signs saying that Santa was inside, waiting to meet you alongside his elves in his grotto. I also loved seeing my own excitement reflected in other children's eyes, how it united us, all spats put aside or forgotten about.

We had decorations at home too, of course. And a Christmas tree wrapped in tinsel, silver and blue. All downstairs.

"We can't make too much fuss, though, we just…can't." Mum would do her utmost to calm me, to stop me from throwing up decorations everywhere. "But, actually, we don't need much, do we? Our house is small. We don't want to swamp it or risk looking garish."

But every child loved garish. Less being more not a concept to be entertained.

Even so, I did my best to follow the rules. If I squealed, I squealed far from home, in the playground or on one of the many walks my mother and I went on. At odd times we did that, we'd walk and walk, even after dark. Our pace wasn't leisurely but quick, hurrying along streets with no obvious destination, with my mother's head bowed as my head was bowed right now, here in this chapel. We didn't talk, because on these occasions, when she did, her voice sounded different, as if it had a crack running right through it.

I tried to be good.

And so did my mother.

My desperate mother, who clung to what she knew, terrified of it falling further apart.

Christmas. For eleven months of the year, I ached for it.

I wanted noise, people to visit and friends to come and play.

I'd been to a friend's house the previous year. It had been the weekend leading up to Christmas, and, oh, it had created a memory to savour!

Sally Goodall was my friend's name, and Diana was her mother. Diana had four children, and she would call me an honorary fifth. She'd treated me like one of her own, enveloping me in a big hug as soon as I'd arrived. She had smelt of Christmas, that's what I remembered thinking, sweet but spicy too. And the noise that surrounded us! Sally's older brother and sisters had friends of their own visit the same day; they seemed to occupy every room. The dog was barking, the cat meowing, and the TV blared.

I sat with Sally at the kitchen table, watching Diana as she bustled about the room, preparing our tea. On the counter was a Christmas cake in a tin.

She must have noticed me watching as she headed over to it with a bottle of something amber in her hand. "I'm feeding it," she said, winking.

"What with?" I asked, amazed that you had to 'feed' a Christmas cake.

"Brandy," she laughingly replied. "I expect your mother does the same." When I remained quiet, she added, "Does she?"

"We make biscuits. Dad doesn't like Christmas cake."

"But he likes biscuits?"

"One or two. Mum takes them up to him with a cup of

tea."

"Up to him?"

"Up to the bedroom."

A frown marred her face. "Oh, I'm sorry. Is your father…unwell?"

I shrugged my shoulders. "I don't know."

Before she could quiz me further, something else amazing happened. The front door slammed, and the kitchen door opened. In waltzed a man, Sally's dad, it had to be, and I say 'waltzed' because, literally, that's what he did, waving his hands in the air.

"Last day of work!" he announced. "The holiday begins right now."

Diana looked just as thrilled as he did at the prospect. She stopped what she was doing and rushed over to hug him. He then turned to Sally and ruffled her hair.

"Who's this?" he said, smiling at me.

"It's my friend," Sally told him. "Lizzie."

"Well, hello, Lizzie! Seems we've got a houseful."

"Haven't we always." Diana rolled her eyes, but I could tell she didn't mind, not really.

"Well," Sally's dad continued, "the more the merrier. It's Christmas, after all." Addressing me again, he added, "Having a sleepover, are you?"

I gazed into his bright blue eyes.

If only. I would have *loved* to stay over.

But I was dropped home that night to a house where curtains were drawn and the world shut out. A house with no siblings and no TV blaring, where you could hear a pin drop.

I loved my mum.

My mum was a good woman.

And my mum loved my dad. *'Til death us do part.*

"Mum!" I yelled upon entering the house. It felt good to raise my voice, it felt…liberating.

Immediately she appeared in the kitchen doorway. "Lizzie!" she said, her voice nothing but an urgent whisper. "What are you doing? You know not to shout."

I raced down the hallway to stand before her. "But, Mum, I've had the best time. It's lovely at Sally's house. There are so many people. It's like a party. Every day. Can Sally come here for tea too? Can we make a Christmas cake? You have to feed it, with brandy! That's a grown-up drink, isn't it? Do we have brandy?"

Mum had her hands in the air, and she kept raising and lowering them. "Lower your voice," she said, she *hissed* at me.

"But, Mum—"

"No, you can't have Sally around here for tea. You know you can't!"

I did know; I'd been told a thousand times. Not Sally, not anyone. Because of Dad. Because he was…sleeping.

Christmas was coming. On that occasion, it would have been my sixth.

Would he make it downstairs? Would he try?

He hadn't for my fifth. It had just been Mum and me, in the kitchen. Mum doing her best, as she always did, for all of us. The memories of my fourth and third were sketchy, but yes, he'd been downstairs, for a while, at least. I could recall a smile on his face as he'd watched me unwrap a present, but it had been a strange smile, one that didn't make you feel especially happy to receive it. As for my second and first Christmas, I had no idea, but there was a picture of me as a baby dressed in a red velvet dress, a Christmassy dress, and I was between my parents, being held by my mum. She was smiling, I was staring wide-eyed, and he was smiling too, that same sad smile.

I had that picture somewhere; it was in this house, in a box, right at the bottom.

The sixth Christmas had come and gone with barely a sign of him.

And then my seventh Christmas approached.

I was getting older, asking more questions.

My father was under the same roof as me, and yet I hardly saw him, barely even crossing paths for bathroom visits. I *heard* him, or, rather, I heard Mum and him whispering together sometimes in the dead of night, when I couldn't sleep and would lie awake listening instead. It sounded like a low hum, barely penetrating the atmosphere, but if I held my breath and listened very, very carefully, if I crept out of bed and made my way over to the wall and leant against it, snatches of words would drift my way.

"It's...all right... No, please...understand."

"Can't...feel so..."

"I know...I know that, darling...here for you."

"Sorry...so..."

"I understand. We...do."

"Sorry."

His voice and hers, sometimes punctuated with a sob – Dad's, never Mum's.

The day I demanded to know wasn't a cold, dull day but a bright, sunny one.

"What's wrong with him, Mum?" Remembering what

Diana had said, I added, "Is he ill?"

We were out of the house, not wandering aimlessly this time but heading to the shops, and so I had no fear we'd be overheard. Rather than answer, she turned her head to the side, away from me. When she eventually spoke, her voice had that familiar crack in it.

"Yes, he's ill," she replied.

At last! A confirmation.

I gulped, felt my voice wobble too. "Is it...is it cancer?"

"Cancer?" There was surprise in Mum's eyes. "How do you know about cancer?"

"We had an assembly at school 'cause one of the teachers has got it. Mrs Laidlaw, who teaches maths. She won't be coming back to school for a while because of it."

Mum shook her head. "Bloody hell, that's a tendency nowadays, isn't it? To overshare. You're kids, for Christ's sake!"

"Mum..." I prompted. "Is that why he never comes out of his room?"

"No, love," she said at last, and her voice held no warmth, only a certain...briskness. "He hasn't got cancer, but he is ill. It's an illness you can't see, but it's there all the same."

"What, Mum? What?" Half of me didn't want to know, but the other half longed to.

Mum stopped then, so I did too. She bent slightly, looked into my eyes, and I noticed how hers had faded, the blue of them so much paler than I'd thought it to be. Had you ever done that, looked into your mother's eyes and seen such sorrow? I had, right there, right then, and thereafter countless times.

She took a deep breath, then exhaled. Every bone in my body felt rigid as I waited.

"You wouldn't understand," she said before straightening and continuing to walk.

Chapter Thirteen

She'd been right; I hadn't understood. I still didn't.

Summer ended, autumn took its turn, then winter descended.

As I've said, my seventh Christmas was approaching, and although the situation in our house had changed somewhat, and not for the better – indoors, I hardly ever saw my mother now either, as she was always upstairs with him – it was impossible to dampen a child's enthusiasm when it came to all things festive.

And so, having finished dinner, which Mum would hurriedly cook then place in front of me – fish fingers, chips and beans, or a variation on it – I would sit at the table and do as I normally did: draw, write or read. I'd draw pictures of a table groaning under the weight of turkey, sprouts, crackers and paper hats. I'd write short stories about magical trips to visit Santa, and I'd read books about the elves in Lapland, who were busy filling sacks with toys they'd handcrafted in their workshops. In short, I created other worlds into which I could escape. This world, with those that hid out of sight, two people in it that whispered only to each other, was a world that was becoming increasingly confusing. I went out of my way to catch glimpses of my father. The door to my parents' bedroom was usually left ajar, and if I knew Mum was busy downstairs, cooking or tidying, I'd push at it slightly. And there he would be, always in stripy pyjamas, sometimes with his back to me or on his side, lying curled like a baby. One time, though, he was on his side and facing me. He had his eyes closed, but he must have sensed me standing there, because he opened them.

"Don't disturb your father," Mum would say, "not for a minute. Leave him to sleep." But it was only characters in a Disney book that needed to sleep for so long.

"Dad," I whispered as his gaze cleared. "Hello."

His eyes lit up, I'm sure they did, briefly.

"Hello, princess," he said, his voice cracked like Mum's sometimes was.

"I miss you," I continued, a declaration that was heartfelt.

He gave a nod of his head, barely perceptible, before closing his eyes again, pulling the cover further up and curling tighter into a ball.

I backed away, leaving the door ajar, hugging to me the words he'd just said.

That I was his princess.

* * *

School had finished for the year.

Mum was waiting for me inside the gates of St Thomas-in-the-Fields in North London, and as I approached, I swear I was fizzing with excitement. Diana, Sally's mum, was there too, standing next to Mum. She was wrapped in a warm, fluffy coat, her cheeks rosy red and a big grin on her face, which widened upon seeing Sally and me.

"Girls! Girls!" she said. "This is it, the countdown. Christmas will soon be here!"

"I can't wait," Sally declared, jumping into the air, arms and legs spread like a starfish.

"Me too," I said, copying her.

How Diana laughed. Mum smiled too, but it was nowhere near as all-encompassing.

"Are we going straight home, Mum?" I asked, not wanting to, not ready to leave this feeling at our door.

"Yes—" she began, but Diana interrupted.

"Why don't we take the girls to the Christmas market off Kilburn High Road for hot chocolate?"

"Yes! Yes! Yes!" Sally roared.

Mum started to shake her head. On seeing this, I roared too.

"Yes! Come on, Sally, let's go." Taking her arm, I steered her towards the gate.

"Liz!" Mum yelled, but I pretended not to hear. This was what you were supposed to do at Christmas, have fun with friends, not return home to a silent house with token decorations and a father who slept both day and night.

It was hot chocolate at the Christmas street market, only that, but it meant so much.

Mum had no option but to follow. When I plucked up the courage to glance back at her, I saw Diana had linked arms with her, as if pulling her along too.

We couldn't find hot chocolate being served among the stalls, so we chose a nearby café instead, went in, selected our table, and the waitress came to take our order.

All the while, I refused to look at Mum, giggling with

Sally instead about the lists we'd made for Santa, wondering how many Beanie Babies he might bring us and whether the latest Tamagotchi might be included too. Sally was also desperate for a board game: *Saved by the Bell*, where you could play pranks on other players. I knew that game; I'd seen it advertised on TV, requiring two to four players, so it was no good for me. Lately, Mum didn't have time for games, or sitting and reading with me like she used to, helping me with spellings. She'd promise, and we would make a start, but then she'd glance upwards towards the ceiling, shake her head and place a hand on my shoulder.

"Just…carry on," she'd say before rising and leaving the room. "I won't be long."

Sometimes, though, she'd only return to put me to bed.

And so, moments like these – hot chocolate in a café with my best friend at the end of school term – I had to grab them. And it was wonderful in that café; it was so cheerful. The waitress wore tinsel around her neck and a silly hat, Christmas tunes were playing, and other kids sat with their mothers too, doing just what Sally and I were doing, huddled together and laughing, hot chocolate or some other treat in front of them.

Despite Mum wanting to go straight home, a quick glance told me that although she was not wholly relaxed, she was at least resigned. Diana was chatting away to her, and Mum was responding in kind. At times she grew quite animated, something of the old Mum coming through, a touch of lightness when she'd become so intense.

She even looked at me and smiled, and I felt warm inside because of it.

I loved my mum. I loved my dad too. I was his princess.

He'd said so.

Despite trying to eke out our hot chocolate, all too soon mugs were empty.

It was time to pay the bill and go. Let others take our place.

Outside the café, Diana addressed Mum.

"Well, that was lovely. We should do it again in the new year, the four of us."

"Yes. Thanks," Mum replied.

"Are you...at home for Christmas or visiting relatives?" Diana persisted.

"We're home," Mum told her. We did have relatives, an uncle and an aunt, some cousins, but they lived too far away to visit. I had no granny or grandad, though. They were 'long gone', Mum had said when I'd asked her about them.

"Lovely," Diana said. "It sounds just right. My house, well, it can get a bit crowded. My husband has five sisters. Five! And they're all really close. They spend a lot of time in each other's pockets, their husbands and children in tow. Honestly, come Christmas Day at ours, there's no room to swing poor Lucy." When both my and Mum's eyes widened, she quickly added, "That's our cat, by the way! So, it'll be the three of you, will it?"

Mum nodded.

Diana sighed dramatically. "One day we'll have a quiet Christmas, just me, my husband and our kids, head off into the sun, maybe, for a barbecue on the beach." A great gale of laughter burst from her. "Doesn't sound right, though, does it? A barbecue on the beach on Christmas Day. Just wouldn't...feel the same. No, I'm envious of you, really I am." Reaching out, she clasped Mum's hand. If she'd noticed her flinch, she didn't mention it. Her voice, though, went from cheerful to something else – sincere. Was that it? Concerned, even. "You have a lovely Christmas, and, you know, if you find yourself at a loose end, call round, have a sherry and a mince pie at ours. The more the merrier. That's what my husband always says, and I agree with him completely. We'd be thrilled to have you visit."

"Thank you. That's very kind of you."

"It's Christmas," Diana insisted. "That's what it's all about, really, isn't it? Love and kindness. Oh, and Jesus, of course." Raising her eyebrows, she added, "Although these kids would have you believe it was all about Barbie!"

Immediately Sally protested. "Mum, we don't play with Barbie dolls! We're far too old."

Diana laughed. "Kids, eh? Gotta love 'em. Look, we're going to have to dash; we have to get some shopping. Feeding the five thousand really does cost a fortune! Happy Christmas," she repeated, grabbing her daughter's hand and beginning to turn from us.

"Happy Christmas," Mum said, but Diana and Sally were already hurrying down the street packed with other shoppers, some looking red-faced and harassed, others with far more beatific expressions on their faces.

I reached for Mum's hand, and together we made our way down the street too, in the opposite direction to Diana and Sally, towards home.

Mum was quiet. She was also anxious. Anxiety seemed to ooze from her, doing its best to penetrate me too. She didn't talk, didn't say a word except to say, "We must hurry."

I didn't want to hurry, though. I wanted to take my time. Visit the shops, especially Mollisons, a huge newsagent set over two floors. Downstairs were the usual newspaper stands, rows of sweets, bags of crisps, and stationery. Upstairs, however, were toys.

As we passed Mollisons, I tried to steer Mum towards it. I wanted to have a look, that's all, not because I was greedy and wanted more toys, but because the staff at Mollisons always went to such trouble to make the upstairs look like something from a Christmas card. Sometimes a canon blasted out fake snow, and tinsel sparkled under old-fashioned lights. The staff would dress as elves, which always made me laugh. They'd hold baskets in their hands, stuffed full of sweets, and they'd hand one out to every child that entered, two if you were lucky, if you could persuade them that you'd been extra good.

"Mum," I said, I begged. "Can't we just go in here before going home?"

It would top off what had been a fantastic day. Christmas lunch in the school canteen, staff and kids all in such high spirits, then hot chocolate in a café with my best friend, and, finally, Mollisons – a high street store that went the extra mile.

"Mum!"

"No! We have to hurry!"

"But why? Why do we? Dad'll be in bed; he'll just be sleeping."

"Don't argue with me, Lizzie."

"But he will! We can go into Mollisons, only for a little while. I want to go, Mum."

"Stop pulling at my hand!"

"Mum!"

"Will you listen to me? I said no."

"But, Mum!"

"NO!"

Abruptly, she let go of my hand. There was such fire in her eyes! She then lifted her hand, fingers held rigid. I stared as if fascinated. What was she going to do? I wondered. Slap me? I'd never been slapped before. Mum said she didn't believe in hitting children. Was she now going to throw that belief aside? Right there and then, in a crowded street?

"Mum!" I breathed as her hand went higher. "MUM!"

As though my raised voice had broken a spell she'd fallen under, she blinked rapidly, gazed at her hand, at how taut it was, as if it was alien to her.

As she lowered it, we both breathed sighs of relief.

She turned and walked hurriedly away.

"We must go home," she said, and this time I followed meekly behind.

Chapter Fourteen

Once inside our house, it was the usual routine. Take shoes
off at the door and place them neatly in the shoebox. Shrug
off coats too and hang them on the peg. We'd hurry straight
through to the kitchen, where certainly I spent most of my
time, as if the front room, the room directly beneath my
parents' bedroom, had faded from existence, even though
that was where the Christmas tree was, the lights not
switched on, not just yet. Sometimes a day or two would go
by without them being switched on. Mum would simply
forget, and, strangely, so would I. I'd draw Christmas trees,
though, sitting at the table in the kitchen, plenty of them,
bright green branches adorned with equally bright red
baubles. I'd *imagine* it sparkling. Maybe somehow,
someway, that had become enough.

In the kitchen, Mum pointed to my books and my
drawing pads.

"Carry on with your reading or some drawing. I'll make
tea in a while. That's if you're hungry after that hot
chocolate."

I was hungry, so I nodded. There was no mention at all
of what had transpired between us, the almost-slap, as if it
had never happened.

"I've got to go and see to your dad," she continued.

"I need to go to the loo—"

"After I've seen to your dad."

As I grabbed at a drawing pad, she set the kettle to boil. He liked his tea hot and sweet, apparently, and she opened the biscuit tin too, selected a star-shaped one and popped it on a plate. It was one I'd made, with white polka-dot icing. I felt pleased she'd picked that one, as if she was trying to make up somehow for what had happened earlier.

"I won't be long," she said. "We'll have sausages and mash tonight. How does that sound? And we can eat it in the living room, in front of the Christmas tree."

She was definitely trying to make it up to me. Not just by her words but her actions too; there was something in her eyes that pleaded with me.

"Okay, Mum," I said, instantly forgiving her.

The tea made, she popped it onto a tray along with the biscuit. As she was about to leave the room, the phone rang.

"Oh," she said, faltering for a second, her gaze travelling between the tray and the cordless phone that hung on the kitchen wall. "I suppose I'd better get it."

On the phone, her voice grew serious. "Oh, at last! Yes, yes, I'm so glad to hear from you. I wasn't expecting you to ring until after Christmas. Absolutely, I'm free to talk. Um…hang on for a moment, will you? My…um…my daughter's here."

Covering the mouthpiece with her hand, she addressed me instead of the caller.

"I have to take this outside, is that okay? You'll stay here?"

I nodded.

"Good girl," she said, and there was a brightness in her voice. "You really are such a good girl."

She opened the back door and, holding the telephone handset, ventured into the garden. It had started to drizzle, but that didn't deter her. Talking to someone on the phone in the garden in the rain was obviously preferable to taking the call in the living room, where voices could drift upwards, or where I could stand in the hallway and listen…

Meanwhile, Dad was waiting for his tea and biscuit.

I could take it up. Place the tray on his bedside table, tiptoe out. Visit the bathroom too. It wasn't such a naughty thing to do. If he was asleep, he wouldn't even notice me. Mum might get cross again, but then, whoever was on the other end of the phone had made her happy, so maybe not. Maybe she'd be grateful I'd saved her the trouble. I was getting bigger now, able to carry a tray, at least, and I was happy to help more. I wanted to.

I picked up the tray, making sure to focus, to concentrate, so I wouldn't spill a drop.

As I entered the hallway, I glanced upwards. It might be that Dad was awake, in which case he might smile at me and call me his princess. I'd like that if he did.

The house wasn't particularly warm; Dad preferred it on the cool side. I didn't mind either, to be honest. I just had to wear an extra jumper if I got cold. It wasn't a big deal.

At the bottom of the stairs, I took my first step, being so careful not to spill anything. Mum would take his dinner up too in the evening, as well as his breakfast in the morning. And lunch. Lately, though, the plates had been coming back with plenty of food still on them, Mum standing at the bin, the knife scraping the plate as she cleared it.

Two steps. Three steps. Up and up I went to reach the top of the narrow staircase.

I looked forward to seeing my father. I missed him. For too long he'd been up here, asleep. If he was awake, perhaps I could ask him about Christmas Day and whether he'd come down for it this year. Maybe…just maybe…he'd come down for Christmas Eve!

As much as I loved Christmas Day, I sometimes wondered if Christmas Eve was better. I didn't know why, maybe because it was the day all that anticipation, that waiting, built to a crescendo. By then, you'd have opened all the windows on your advent calendar, so you only had the clock to watch, the big day drawing tantalisingly closer.

Wouldn't it be brilliant if he came downstairs for Christmas Eve and joined us in the kitchen? It would be the icing on the cake. A thought that caused me to stifle a giggle, imagining Diana and the Christmas cake that she fed. I wondered what brandy tasted like and whether a big fat slice could get you drunk. Diana had said Mum and I were welcome to come over before Christmas, to 'pop in'. I hoped Mum would accept her offer and, rather than a mince pie, she'd cut some of that cake so I could try it and see.

Not far to go now. My parents' room was opposite mine, then there was another room. It was tiny; Mum called it a box room, and certainly there were boxes in it, full of spare things, she said. Things that might come in handy someday.

The door to that room was closed, as it always was. My door was closed too – I must have shut it on the way out this morning, although I didn't remember doing so.

It was so quiet upstairs. It was quiet throughout the house, but up here, I don't know, it was as if the house were holding its breath somehow, not daring to disturb Dad.

Because it mustn't, and nor must I. Dad must be allowed to rest. I'd been told that for so long. Had it ever been noisy here? Had it ever been just a little like Diana's house, laughter, if not constant, at least not a total stranger? The *three of us* laughing, not two.

Poor Mum. She tried her best, for me and Dad, but maybe…just maybe…more for Dad.

He was lucky to have her. We were all lucky to have each other. Some children didn't have parents; they had to live with aunts or uncles or grandparents, or another couple would come along and be their mummy and daddy. Adoption. We'd learnt about it in school, about all the different families there were in the world. But I had my mum, and even though I barely saw him, I had my dad too. I was lucky. And I might get luckier still if Dad agreed to come downstairs.

Dad's door was ajar. It always was. Funny, really, because if he needed peace so much, you'd think he'd want it closed.

Just before pushing it open, a random thought occurred.

What if we had a cat?

A kitten, soft and cute.

That would be such fun! I wouldn't feel so alone, then. When I was left downstairs in the kitchen to draw, to read, to write, the cat would be with me, purring. It would never leave my side. Oh, how my heart soared! A cat would be the answer to everything. Just as Mum was largely Dad's companion, it would be mine. Was it too late to add it to my Christmas list? Of course not; Santa wouldn't read it until Christmas Eve. I had a few days yet. A black-and-white cat, or a ginger one. What would I name it? I'd have to think carefully, not rush it. A name was a very important thing. You carried it with you through life.

I was still thinking about the cat as I placed my shoulder against the door and pushed it open, the tray still carefully balanced. I'd heard miracles happened at Christmas. If there was a kitten waiting for me on Christmas morning underneath the tree in the living room, a bow around its neck, pink for a girl, blue for a boy, that would be a miracle indeed.

A little kitten, just for me. A playmate, a friend. Some life in this house.

Still trying not to spill Dad's tea, I decided to announce my arrival, just in case he was awake but lying on his side with his back to me, staring at the wall.

"Dad, it's me. Mum made you some tea, and I made you a biscuit. Dad," I continued, pushing the door wider, my eyes all the while on the brown liquid, proud that I hadn't spilt it, not one single drop, and hoping he'd be proud of me too. "I was thinking of adding to my Christmas list. I want a kitten. Wouldn't that be a good idea? A family pet—"

When I was met with silence, I raised my eyes.

Sometimes it was hard to believe your eyes. It was like…you couldn't trust them.

Was I really seeing what was before me, or was this a dream, a nightmare?

It couldn't be true.

It couldn't be.

I blinked several times. One…two…three…

Willed the scene to change.

Oh, please. Please.

For a Christmas miracle of another kind to occur.

Don't let it be true.

But the scene remained the same.

Dad's feet were dangling in front of me, stripy pyjamas hanging loose on such a thin body. And his head was to the side, at the oddest of angles.

His eyes weren't closed but open. They couldn't see me, though, couldn't see anything.

Not anymore.

We had to be quiet in this house. Dad didn't like noise. Noise upset him.

But the scream that tore loose from my chest, the clatter of the tray and its contents as it flew first into the air, then landed at my feet, was loud enough to be heard from the garden.

Although still screaming, I registered my name being called.

"Lizzie! Lizzie, what's going on? What is it? Oh God, what is it?"

Mum was now behind me, her screams joining mine as she discovered what I had.

There was so much noise.

But Dad wouldn't mind.

Not one bit.

Dad was dead. He'd hanged himself.

Chapter Fifteen

Oh, it was so cold in the chapel. And it was so quiet, up until now.

Now there was a low moan, a keening. Had a gale got up outside? And, just like the mist, would it find its way through the cracked panes and the eaves to move stealthily throughout the house? It was a strange sound. Not one I'd heard before. Low but getting louder. Not a cry of lamentation, this contained something other than that. Anger.

I straightened my back and lowered my hands to my lap.

The cry wasn't external to me. Only now did I realise that. It was coming from deep within, a howl from a darkened pit, that had lain dormant for so long.

My eyes widened as my mouth stretched.

Dad had killed himself!

He'd killed himself, and I'd been the one to find him!

I was fully moaning now.

That image of his legs dangling, his eyes bulging imprinted on my mind. Forever.

And Al knew nothing about it.

My friends knew nothing about it.

My past. My history.

Some things you wrote down, some things you told others. And some things you never breathed a word about.

It was a secret. Mum had insisted.

Abruptly, I stood up, the moan never faltering, accompanied by tears now that burst from my eyes to race down my cheeks, drip, drip, dripping to the floor.

A suicide.

The shame of it.

I had to get out of this chapel, with its stone walls, stone altar and stone bench. Escape the coldness that drenched not just this room and this building but me as well, a part of my heart, such a large part, frozen. Now, though, it was as if some kind of thaw had set in, unbidden, unwelcome; rather, it was sudden, and it was shocking, threatening a deluge.

I'd closed the door to the chapel after I'd entered, but now I pulled hard to open it. Back in the sixth bedroom, I stood for a moment, just to catch my breath, then hurled myself onwards through the darkness and into the dimly lit landing with its hissing, flickering lights.

Still that terrible keening filled my ears as I stood at the top of the holly-entwined staircase, as I gazed not to the left of me, to the room where so much pacing had occurred, but forwards, to rest on shiny green leaves and red berries.

I wanted them off there.

I wanted them gone.

Christmas. Always such an exciting time.

Why did I insist on clinging to that lie?

The keening became something else as I moved forwards, a roar, both of my hands out before me tearing at the holly, its spiked edges biting back as if in protest, but I didn't care.

I was in no mood to worry about more wounds inflicted.

Because nothing – *nothing* – could compare to the hurt I already felt.

I ripped the holly off the ribbons, stamped it beneath my feet, intent on grinding it to pulp, squashed red berries leaking blood. Down I went, stair by stair, a raging thing yet at the same time methodical, ensuring nothing escaped me. I wanted no reminder at all.

At the bottom of the littered stairs, stairs I'd once intended to sweep down as something glamorous, not this raging beast that had been let loose, there was further handiwork to mock me. Stars and snowflakes, paper chains and tinsels.

The roar was replaced by a laugh, harsh and brittle.

They all had to come down. Every last one.

The ceiling was high. I felt too drunk on anger to climb a ladder. A broom would do.

I rushed through the darkened corridor and into a kitchen that was just as dark, straight towards the scullery, where the broom was kept with its long wooden handle.

There was mist at the window. Always, there was mist at the window. Isolating me. Imprisoning me. Ensuring that I was alone with her. And not just her but with memories too. This unrelenting quiet had provoked them, caused them to rise upwards, to tumble into my mind. *Oh, at last! Yes, yes…so glad to hear from you. I wasn't expecting…until after Christmas. Absolutely, I'm free to talk…hang on for a moment…my daughter's here.*

The laughter and roaring having ceased – for how long, I had no idea – Mum's voice was as clear as if she were standing there beside me. The brightness in it that I now knew to be hope. Later, years later, she'd told me who was on the phone that night…a counsellor, an expert. Finally, she'd asked for help. And help had been offered. Too late, though. Much too late.

I grabbed the broom, only my breathing heavy in my ears now, punctuated with sobs.

Back in the hallway, the stars and snowflakes stood out against the darkness like a silhouette in negative.

Lifting the broom handle, I hit out at them. They swayed, they dodged me at first, as if we were involved in a game and they could win.

They couldn't.

As well as the fire that raged inside me, there was determination.

The decorations were coming down.

No more merry twinkling. No more…charade.

Silently they floated to the floor on invisible wings.

And that enraged me further.

I stamped on them, just as I'd stamped on the holly. I tore them apart with my hands until they were unrecognisable, bits of ruined paper that could float no more. I also grabbed at the tinsel – silver, red and blue – and ran my hand down the spine of it, imagining it as some monstrous snake that wriggled, trying to get away from me as I picked it clean, as I stripped it of its gaiety to leave behind something pitiful instead.

As for that snowman, standing mute beside the door, I would wipe his stupid grin off his stupid face, battering him over and over to leave just a deflated plastic sack.

Only when I'd destroyed everything did I stop to survey my handiwork.

Over. It was all over. What should never have been. Not here.

Just the living room to see to now, where the Christmas tree was.

I'd begun striding towards it when a sound interrupted my progress: 'Jingle Bells'.

It was my phone, the ringtone, one freshly loaded. After all, 'tis the season.

Someone was trying to contact me.

Al?

The song ended.

Then it began again.

Oh, jingle bells, jingle bells,
Jingle all the way.
Oh! What fun it is to ride
In a one-horse open sleigh, hey!

It ended.

It began.

It would be Al. 'Where are you? What are you doing? Are you okay?' Those would be the questions on his lips. My answer: 'No. I am not okay. I haven't been since I was seven.'

No way was I going to answer it. I was on a mission.

As soon as I could, though, I'd get my phone, if only to change that damned ringtone! There was another festive tune that could take its place, one with lyrics far more apt, that spoke blatantly about the lie of Christmas, about a dream sold to every child – that declares, right at the end, we get the Christmas we deserve.

Had we deserved what Dad did to us?

He'd had a family that loved him. Mum had loved him.

She'd been devoted to him, above me, even. His lover, his wife, his nurse, the one who'd shielded him and who'd failed him.

That's how she'd seen it. And she'd never been the same again.

She had carried on looking after me, delivering the child into adulthood. She'd lived, she'd breathed, but all the while there had been a disease inside her, and it ate away at her, cell by cell. Some might call it cancer. But not me. I knew it for what it truly was. Heartbreak. My father had deprived us of him, and in doing so, he'd taken my mother too. After him, she'd never been whole. Like he hadn't been whole. Like I couldn't be.

Dead inside. A shadow.

"Why, Dad?"

The voice that cried out was mine, but there was such a whine in it, like that of a child.

One hand flew to my mouth to smother any further sound.

And then I heard it: the pacing from upstairs. And it pricked yet another memory, one I'd suppressed.

Dad hadn't always lain in bed; sometimes he would pace. Just like Josephina had paced.

Up and down, up and down.

And *that* was why Mum hadn't liked us to sit in the living room, when we'd have been perfectly capable of sitting there in silence. She hadn't wanted me to hear the pacing.

But I had. And at some point, it had embedded itself deep into my psyche.

Pacing. Up and down. Up and down. Steady. Measured.

One, two, three… One, two, three… Back and forth. Back and forth.

A torturous rhythm.

I fell into the same one, my feet crunching over spoilt paper and tinsel strands.

My breathing followed a similar pattern. In and out. In and out. One, two, three… One, two, three… Keeping perfect time with Josephina and…Joseph. Yes, that had been my father's name. Joseph. The reason I'd caught my breath when my fingers had traced the name on the grave. Thinking for a moment…just a moment…it was him, not her. Joseph. Oh, the irony! A name uttered so much at Christmas too – Jesus, Mary and Joseph, a family, as we had been a family. One that had also been torn apart.

One, two, three… One, two, three…

Focus. Walk. Don't think. Give your fevered brain a break. Just try not to think anymore.

That's it.

Walk. Back and forth. To and fro. Up and down. Walk.

Like Joseph, like Josephina. Two separate people. One and the same.

The same malady, the same fate.

Entwined.

My hands were now agitated, nails scratching at skin that was already bloodied.

His illness, what if it's a part of me in more ways than one?

Jingle bells, jingle bells…

My ringtone snapped me back to reality.

Al. Ringing again and again. Breaking off. Calling back straightaway.

My husband. A man who believed the lies I'd fed him,

that my dad had had a problem with addiction, that he'd been unfaithful to Mum. Eventually, she'd had enough and kicked him out. We'd had nothing more to do with him. Cut all contact. Not hearing another thing, only that he'd died years later when I was in my teens. And no, we hadn't attended the funeral nor enquired where he was buried. Oh, I'd painted such a picture of him! Me, who loved to draw, read and write. I'd created a villain of another kind. Destroyed an unbearable truth.

My dad had committed suicide. Because we weren't enough for him. Me and Mum.

Jingle bells…

Damn that ringtone!

I hated it!

And damn Christmas.

One more gesture towards it: the tree. Standing beyond in that cold room, that dark room, with only the mist at the windows for company.

That had to go too.

Chapter Sixteen

The lights on the tree were on. Gently flashing.

Standing just inside the door, I frowned.

I didn't remember having switched them on.

But there they were, twinkle, twinkle, little star-shaped lights creating such a glow.

Welcoming, almost.

I inhaled a deep breath. Roared yet again as I exhaled.

The mockeries, would they never stop coming?

Would the memories I barely acknowledged ever stop plaguing me?

How late was it? I had no idea.

Had Al finished with his bosses? Been welcomed deeper into the fold?

Who cared? I didn't, not in that moment.

I wanted only to rush forwards and tear the lights from the socket. I hadn't switched them on; I was certain of it. I hadn't even been in the living room that night. Instead of following my impulse to seize the lights, though, I fell to my knees, almost in an act of prayer, though no stone altar lay before me.

"Why'd you do it, Dad? Why?"

That time he'd called me princess, I had gazed into his

eyes, and he had gazed back into mine. It wasn't the first time he'd said that – more memories echoed in the recesses of my mind – there'd been other times, but long, long ago. I had gazed into his eyes, and I had seen something… Love. Yes, there'd been that. But something else too. Something I would see in my own eyes if I was to rush right now to the cloakroom and look into the mirror over the sink. Weariness. He was tired. So tired.

"That's why he sleeps so much," Mum had said. "Because he's tired."

An illness of another kind. One you couldn't see. That so few had sympathy for.

And, by and large, I'd accepted his tiredness. How strange it was, how extreme.

But a child never stopped hoping.

A child dreamed it would all get better, that dreams really did come true.

And that Christmas was indeed a time for miracles.

Rarely was a child without hope.

But as we grew, as the years ticked by, we became something quite different, and hope faded.

That tree. That bloody cheerful tree.

Unable to hold back any longer, I lunged forwards, hands as well as knees scrabbling across the floor, watched as a teardrop splashed onto the boards in front of me and then another. How they twinkled too, perfect pearls.

I pushed upwards to stand on my feet and lunged again. I'd tear that tree down, just like I'd torn everything else in this house down. This was the last bastion, the archetypal icon. I'd smash every fucking bauble on it!

And whoever stood in the mist could watch.

Is it you, Josephina? Can you see me, can you? What about you, Dad, can you see me too from wherever you are? Mum, wasn't this fury in you too? Except for that almost-slap, you were always so calm, so...contained. Didn't you ever want to do what I'm doing now? Rage against it all?

When the carol singers had come to our door during my eighth Christmas – they'd never come before, as if they'd known not to – we had stood in the hallway, Mum and me, wondering what to do, whether we could open the door, whether it'd be all right to do so. We hadn't, though. We'd continued to stand there until their voices died away, then Mum had turned and gone back into the kitchen, leaving me with a cold certainty: we would *never* open the door to carol singers and well-wishers at Christmas, the likes of Diana and Sally. That invite to their house would not be reciprocated. Because somehow, in some way, Dad remained. Whilst still in that hallway of old, my eyes had travelled upwards to stare at the ceiling. Christmas: not an exciting time, it was a terrible time, the worst.

The very worst.

All through my remaining childhood.

Although dead, Dad was more present than ever.

Why'd you do it? Why?

I found my voice, a thing as wrecked and as tortured as the tree before me, my hands still grabbing at it, pulling, crushing and smashing.

"Why'd you have to do it at Christmas?!"

It seemed crueller that he had.

"What was your reason?"

Because I'd never been told; it had never been discussed. All that Mum had said, that she'd repeated over and over, was no one needed to know what had truly happened. We could mask the truth. Make up another reason. Protect his memory. No one had to realise how powerless we were to make him want to stay.

An invisible illness, as I've said. One that was sometimes scorned.

Even by me.

A tree bereft of all that had once adorned it was a pitiful sight. Good. That's what I wanted, what I sought. It stood there still, as tall as me, defiant despite its nakedness. And so, my hands back on it, pine needles stinging as much as the holly had, biting deeper into cuts, I pulled it forwards and brought it crashing to the floor, ending that defiance.

What time was it? I still had no idea. Thankfully, 'Jingle Bells' was silent. There was quiet once more – and mist. I walked towards the window, placed my hands against cold glass.

You're everywhere, aren't you, Josephina? Out there. In here. All around me. Just like Dad. He never left, and nor did you.

Pacing again. So faint. And an echo, a whisper.

Eventually, I turned towards the tree. It shouldn't be in my house; it should be outside, in the soil, in the big wide open, reaching for the sky. It was just another casualty of Christmas, as Mum was, as I was. All part of a lie. A great big fat, dirty lie.

Al had believed me when I'd fed the lies to him about my father.

Hadn't even blinked an eyelid. Why would he?

My friends had believed me too. Again, no reason not to.

And eventually, *I'd* started to believe it. Especially when Mum had passed, when there was not a soul left to know otherwise. That look in her eyes – so haunted – vanquished.

But this house and how quiet it was, other than the pacing and echo of voices, had brought it all crashing back. Every painful bit. Carfax House. Where lives had been lived, one that had run parallel to my father's, the memory of it, the same emotions.

All of it being relived through my presence here. Its conduit.

The pacing was so faint I had to strain to hear it. The echo just that, resounding from far, far away.

I kicked aside the carnage at my feet as I turned my back on the mist, my breath heavy as my chest heaved. The heaters must have flicked off again, as it was icy, the cold creeping in through the cracked windowpanes every bit as much as I imagined the mist did. What would Al make of this? As the song said, it would take some time, but he'd get here, get his feet on holy ground. Holy? I almost laughed. Chris Rea had sung another song, one more apt. 'The Road to Hell'. That was it. A road I knew.

A minute later and I was outside the living room, back in the entrance hall. The darkness wasn't intense, not anymore, as if mist was indeed rising within, just like old memories had risen.

I drew my gaze to yet more carnage, litter that lay like hunchbacked shadows. And movement caught my eye. No surprise that it should.

There was a figure in midair, dangling.

Just over the grand stairwell.

Which one of us was it?

Because it could be the future I was looking at, not the past.

Not Josephina, not Joseph, but me.

"NO!"

The broom was propped up against the stairs, and I ran to it, grabbed it, then started up those stairs, closer to the figure, holding the broom aloft all the while, hitting out at it whilst screams rose, more of them, and the question I had no answer to.

"Why? Why? Why?"

I was as desperate as a child at a party game, hitting at a piñata. It wasn't something sweet I wanted, however, but something as bitter as the truth.

"Why, Dad? Why?"

He was a man I'd barely known, and yet he had left his indelible mark, filled me with regret, with sadness and with shame. How I hit out at that shadow that could be him, or her, or me, clutching that broom with all my might. A shadow that had remained in my mind from the minute I'd first seen it, when I'd realised I was no one's princess, not anymore.

"You…you…bastard! How could you? You destroyed everything."

Al had been bemused that I'd wanted to go to Carfax House before Christmas. That I couldn't wait. "You always go to so much effort at Christmastime," he'd said. "You're like a kid, how excited you get. I don't know anyone else who makes as much effort."

True. All true. As an adult, I'd embraced the season. I'd festoon the flat in decorations; I'd organise one Christmas gathering after another, both at the flat and in restaurants and bars around London. I'd desperately squeeze everything I could from it. Come into my own. A party queen. At

Christmastime. *Only* at Christmastime.

I'd go to so much effort...but to do what? To mask the memory further? Exorcise it?

And I thought I'd succeeded. But Carfax House had other ideas.

With a final, almighty swing of the broom, the shadow at last dispersed, inky tendrils dissipating before vanishing. The space before me was empty, as hollow as I was inside.

After all my exertions, I had to bend over, and it took a long while for my breathing to regulate, for yet more sobs to be stifled, for silence to reign yet again.

Silent night, holy night.

That's what the hymn said, what it insisted despite my thoughts to the contrary.

I straightened up, let go of the broom. It had done its work. Progressing to the top of the stairs, I stood at the window as I'd done before and stared outwards, towards the grave.

That's why Josephina was buried there, because she had taken her own life also, forsaken the right to lie in consecrated ground. Not that it had mattered to her. To her, there'd been nothing sacred about life or death. All she'd wanted was...nothingness.

A figure in the mist. There was one. Drifting. Endlessly. Pacing. Endlessly. And praying. A figure that was turning slowly towards me.

Before we could face each other fully, however, I turned away and walked past lights that only flickered and hissed at me, into the sixth bedroom and to the chapel.

Crossing the room, I grasped the cold iron ring and pushed at it. On this occasion, the door opened without protest.

It was time, that was why, to listen to the whispers more carefully.

Crossing over to the altar, I knelt, the stone so cold, so hard beneath me. My hands coming together, I rested them beneath my chin as I had before when sitting on the stone bench. Just as my feet had kept perfect pace downstairs with the walking to and fro, now my lips moved in time with the echoes, with the whispers etched into the atmosphere.

That was my story.

This is hers.

Chapter Seventeen

Is there anyone who will listen to me? Who will understand? Is that too much to hope for? I fear it is. For how can someone understand me if I cannot understand myself? My body contains my heart and my soul. The former I can hear beating sometimes in the dead of night, when the people I share shelter with beneath this roof, my family, are asleep. When all is quiet at Carfax House, when even the animals outside are at slumber. It is only I that lie awake, hour after hour. Endless hours! I listen to nothing but the beating of my heart, its steady rhythm. And a thought enters my head. Always the same thought. Always dreadful.

I wish that my heart would stop beating, that it would become as quiet as this house around me at this hour.

My soul is tarnished. It is ungrateful. Damned.

The sun rises, as it always does. Day after day after day. And sometimes it is bright; it shines down upon this corner of land my father calls glorious, that my mother does too.

"Come," she will say, entering my room and urging me to dress, cajoling me with that sweet, soft voice of hers, "let's walk in the garden. The roses are perfectly splendid at this time of year. They're in full bloom. Pinks, reds and yellows, such pretty colours, the yellow especially. It's so…cheerful. Come, Josephina, and walk with me."

Not wishing to offend her, I rise and do as she desires, playing my part. How she loves the roses, devoting so much time to tending them. The garden brings her such joy. Today, it might do the same for me. Hope springs eternal. But is this hope? Or desperation?

It really is such a glorious day. A summer's day. The sky is blameless, the brightest of blues with not a cloud in sight. She is right. The roses will look splendid; they will smell delightful. I will enjoy today, I will. I will see what she sees: the beauty in everything.

Mother takes my arm as we enter the garden, gravel beneath our feet finally giving way to the softness of grass. The grounds are extensive. "It is our sanctuary," my father says. "All that we need is here."

And yet often he is away, staying over in London, working with his business associates to provide us with this haven. My elder brother works beside him, and so it is Mother and I who have the house to ourselves, to pass the hours here, quiet hours that fade into a single expanse of tranquillity.

"Almost there," Mother says as we continue to walk arm in arm, one hand reaching out to pat mine as if in reassurance. "We're almost there."

The sun is warm on my face; it caresses me. And yet, as my feet reach a certain spot, a shiver runs through me, and I am enveloped in coldness. Visibly, I start.

"Dear?" Mother says, noticing. "Are you quite well?"

I nod, although, strangely, I remain cold. It holds me as if we were in deepest winter, not summer at all. I look down at the ground and see nothing but grass, a daisy scattered here and there. I shake my head, dismiss what has happened. It is of no consequence. The cold is something I am used to. The warmth never lasts for long.

"Here we are!" says Mother, and gracing her face is the widest smile, her dark eyes shining. "Look at the blooms, Josephina, aren't they dazzling?"

A panoply of colour! Each separate bush that stands is nothing less than abundant, each bud so artfully shaped, their petals delicate and numerous. The fragrance that emanates is reminiscent of nasturtium, violet and cloves.

Mother's rose garden. Her pride and her joy. Here, there are no weeds in sight, no stray daisies. Nothing must be allowed to taint this sacred ground, to ruin the perfection. She wants me to love it as much as she does. To take as much pride.

And I try. I really do.

But I simply cannot see what she sees. I cannot feel those same emotions.

My soul is tainted, I know it is. It is…wrong. I am wrong. Through and through.

Because like the hours, the colours before me fade so quickly to become grey. And accompanying that heady scent is a tinge of something else, something…ruined.

Mother pats my arm once more before disengaging and making her way to the largest bloom, one that is a pearlised pink, that she insists shimmers before us.

"We won't pick this one," she says. "It would be sacrilege to do so. Instead, we'll pick some smaller blooms, for the house and for your room. Wouldn't that be lovely? Having something beautiful to wake to every morning."

Something that might inspire me is what she means. For she is fully aware there is such melancholy within me, and although she tries to help, she is perplexed, just as I am perplexed. From where did it come? At what age did it start? I am a young woman now, aged twenty-four, but I cannot remember a day it hasn't been there, inside me, heaving and writhing, sucking the colour from everything, the joy, creating a void in which I alone stand.

Mother is wearing her apron, and in the pocket are scissors that she uses to cut several blooms.

"Josephina, hold them, dear. Be careful of the thorns. Don't make yourself bleed."

But I am always bleeding. Right here, right now, in this summer sunshine, my heart feels as it always does, as if it were haemorrhaging.

The roses are placed in my room, in a small vase. And every morning I indeed wake to look at them. So pert and pretty, pale pink petals soon begin to curl, to turn brown at the edges, to drop onto the sideboard, to wither yet more.

Everything has its time.

As the roses in my bedroom wilt, so do the ones that remain on the bushes outside. Summer gives way to autumn, the greens and golds of nature's palette no more; instead, leaves turn darker, browns and yellows that aren't as cheerful.

In the house, the fires are made up. This is a big house with plenty of rooms, and it is important, Mother says, not to let the cold sink its claws in too deep, for then it becomes difficult to loosen its grip. It will creep into every corner and every recess and lurk there.

When she says this, she says it with a smile, but I want to reach out and grab her, look into her eyes, scream and yell, tell her that that is how I feel! Coldness has sunk too deep within me; there is no vestige of warmth left. It is gone, all gone. And I don't know why.

But, of course, I refrain. Turn away instead, lower my head, pretend I am busy tending to some other matter. I have already said I do not want to upset Mother or any of my family. It is the last thing I would wish to do. But I'm inflicting pain nonetheless, because I catch the look in Mother's eyes as I turn away, her worry and concern, notice a hand that itches to reach out, to console me, but knows better. There is no consolation to be had.

This house was built in 1868 by a well-regarded architect: Simon Lilley. We are not the first people to live here; the family before us were here for quite some time until their circumstances changed, but now it is ours, the Standens'. How long it stays in our family remains to be seen. My brother, whose name is John, adores London. When he returns here, he tries to disguise it, but he is restless and looks forward to leaving again at the earliest opportunity. He has even tried to persuade me to accompany him. Father has too, all of us visiting London as a family.

"You would love it," John insists, "it is vibrant, it heaves with atmosphere. There are fine shops, fine restaurants. There are trains! They run in the tunnels beneath your feet. You have to see it to believe it. There are lamps everywhere too, all along the Embankment. Not gas lamps but electric. Oh, Josephina! You really would love it. There is light everywhere!"

And I wonder about that, the light, and there being so much of it. Would it indeed be something to see? Would it…make a difference?

"Next time we go, come with us. Please."

His voice is soft, just as cajoling as Mother's.

My brother loves me; my parents do too. And I love them, but I do not want to go to London, not even to see the lights. I shake at the very thought, and my breathing becomes heavier.

Again, I have to turn from eyes that are so confused, so sorrowful.

When Lilley built this house, he built a small chapel leading off from one of the bedrooms. No one knows why, whether it was requested or a detail that merely took his fancy. After all, Lilley was also an architect renowned for adding unusual features, a hidden nook, perhaps, where one could read a book in private, or a closet that leads into a smaller, more secret closet. But a chapel? To our knowledge, this is something quite unique. It is just a small room, but one with an oval window and a stone altar, a place to kneel – also made from stone – and a stone bench. The room that leads to it is not one used regularly. Even guests, when they have stayed in the past, are placed elsewhere. An empty room, it is only I that enters it because it is only I that ever feels the need.

When the pain and confusion in John's or Mother's eyes becomes too much, it is there I go, through that room to the one beyond to bend my knee, my head in prayer.

To ask again: Why? Why? Why?

No one wants an answer more than the person who suffers.

My lips move, my heart yearns.

I bleed. All the time, I bleed, and it is nothing but anguish.

Winter arrives, and Mother is excited.

Again, she enters my room and begs me to rise from bed, where I am spending more and more time, whole days, entire weeks, allowing them to drift by without me, for it is better that way, that this malaise I'm inflicted with is kept from others.

"We're to have a party!" she declares. "Father has agreed, and so preparations must start as soon as possible. A party, Josephina! We shall invite all we know. They will come from

London because of it. It will be such a grand affair. Something to celebrate the Christmas season! We will both need new dresses, jewellery and…and… Oh! There is so much we need to do, so many plans to make. We mustn't waste a moment."

A party for my benefit. Potential suitors to be asked, I'm sure of it. A husband-to-be. Perhaps he will make me happy, Mother thinks, succeed where they have failed.

No!

I do not want it.

But Mother is like a hurricane and cannot be stopped. If I fail to rise from bed, she will drag me from it, I am certain. And so I have to try. Have to summon up energy when I feel bone weary, find enthusiasm where there is none.

Christmas is coming. A time for gaiety, laughter. I have to try…

So much to prepare. A list that is endless. The house is akin to a hurricane too, so many coming and going: florists, caterers and designers. We are having a party, for Christmas, for me, when before there's only been silence, one I have forced upon us.

Yes, I've seen doctors. But not too many. My parents are wary, perhaps fearing my incarceration. Fearing it and yet half wanting it, I am sure. A husband is an altogether kinder way to offload me, and my parents and brother are kindness itself.

The morning of the party dawns, cold and frosty. A grand house, a grand affair. More people coming and going, an endless stream, their faces so intent as busy hands work.

Even I can see how dazzling Carfax House is. It has truly come to life, it glitters, a house made for an occasion such as this. And I am to glitter too.

Oh, the dress Mother has chosen for me! I've had countless fittings to ensure it fits me perfectly. My dark hair is tended to, *tiny rosebud jewellery placed within it – a cheerful colour, yellow – and around my neck is fastened a string of pearls, a family heirloom.*

The day dawns, the hours pass, and evening arrives.

I stand in front of the mirror, eyes roaming over every inch of the vision before me.

I am to leave my room soon. Everyone who has been invited is here.

I will sweep down the stairs for all to behold.

It is Christmas, and Mother has gone to such effort. She was in my room just moments ago, admiring me.

"Remember to smile," she said before leaving. "Just…remember to smile."

She was not merely asking; she was pleading.

Chapter Eighteen

Silence.

No more music, no more laughter, no more sharp intakes of breath as I indeed descended the stairs with a smile on my face. No murmurings of appreciation. No nods of approval. Not anymore. It is over. The party has ended.

And I am alone. In my room. Pacing. Walking back and forth. One, two, three… One, two, three… My hands together, skin rubbing against skin. Nails scratching.

A disaster. That's what it was. As is everything that involves me. But I tried, I really did. I saw how hard Mother had worked. I wanted to please her. Made so many promises to myself. I'd smile. I'd laugh. I'd whirl when I danced, act coquettish as women my age sometimes do. I'd be demure, gaze up from beneath half-closed eyelids, capturing the heart of every eligible young man in attendance. I would be spoilt for choice!

And Mother would be so proud of me, Father and John too.

I was young and considered beautiful. I was privileged. A bright future lay ahead! After securing a husband, I would have children and a house to call my own, as big if not bigger than Carfax House. I would shake off this silliness, shed it as you would a coat. All I needed to do was make that decision. Not hide or be sad anymore. This party was such a grand affair; it would mark the end of one chapter and the beginning of another.

Except it did not. It could not.

Oh, everyone was in a fine mood! The excitement so palpable that you felt you could reach out and grab it, hug it to you, hold it fast. And I did that; I wrapped it around myself, endeavoured to drown in the happiness of others. I smiled. I laughed. I danced! My card was full, young man after young man lining up to dance me around the room. Outside it was cold, and the cheeks of men and women were still fetchingly rosy from arrival. A fire was roaring in the room in which we danced and in other rooms too. Mulled wine and cider were served, and champagne in wide-rimmed glasses.

Musicians had been hired, and the fashionable tunes of the day played. I barely listened to music, but I could understand those that did. It lifted the atmosphere. Even those that stood beside the dancing couldn't help but tap their toes as they conversed.

One man in particular was keen to dance with me, over and over.

A friend of John's, he was from London and two years older than me. A bachelor. Seeking a wife. Occupying an excellent position at the bank, he was also handsome.

"John talks of you endlessly," he told me, such eagerness in his bright blue eyes. "I've been so looking forward to meeting you. Will you dance with me again?"

As we waltzed, I caught sight of John, a look of pure delight on his face.

When the dance ended, I was breathless.

"Would you like a refreshment?" he asked. "Some champagne?"

I nodded. I'd already had one glass, but I could manage

another.

"*Come with me,*" *he said.*

There were so many people! So much laughter! Carfax House was bursting with it.

I could hear my mother's voice and turned to search for her. She was talking to a group of people, holding court, so animated. Who were these people? I wondered. There were so many I didn't recognise. Father's friends and John's. London people. Society. Come here to Leicestershire, to the countryside.

I realised the young man at my side was talking. "It's cold outside, but…"

We'd be alone; that's what he meant. Away from the crowds.

What would be the harm?

Once outside, he removed the black jacket he wore and draped it across my shoulders. I smiled again at such a chivalrous action.

"*We will only be moments,*" *he assured me.*

"*What about you?*" *I asked. "Aren't you cold?"*

"*Oh, I'm more than happy,*" *he replied. Samuel was his name, Samuel Marks. As I've said, he was a fine man, a catch.* "*I really am so happy to meet you.*"

"*And I'm happy to meet you.*"

"*You don't come to London much?*"

"*I prefer it here.*"

"*But you'd love London! There is so much to see!*"

I must have stared curiously at him, because he hurried on, telling me about art galleries, museums and exhibitions.

"*And there are trains that run beneath your feet, apparently,*" *I added. "John has told me. And light. There is light.*"

"*There is! You simply must come and visit. Or…*" *He*

faltered, was shy suddenly.

"Or?"

"Or allow me to visit you here?"

"Oh," was all I said in reply, was all I could manage.

"Would you?" he persisted. "Allow me, I mean? I do so enjoy your company."

"I...I..." This was the aim of the night, why the party had been organised, Christmas just an excuse. But now that it had become something of a reality, that I had a suitor indeed, it was only panic that bloomed in my chest. Here was a man who would dance with me, who enjoyed being with me, who didn't know me at all.

"No!" The word was out before I could stop it. More followed. "That cannot be."

His expression was one of surprise.

"We've danced together," he said. "Several times. You're here with me now, standing outside with me, where the air is so cold. Yet still you came. John has told me so much about you that I feel..." He cleared his throat. "Josephina, we are well suited, I am certain of it. In short, you are everything I expected and more. You are so beautiful."

He reached out a hand to lay upon my arm, nothing more, but panic choked me.

"NO!" I repeated, I screamed. "John has told you nothing but lies."

"Josephina—"

My hand shot out and knocked his glass flying, sending it upwards into the air, golden beads of champagne drenching us both.

"What the deuce..." he began, but quickly his voice died away, and he looked at me in horror as I stood there, shaking so

violently that his jacket fell from my shoulders. "What is wrong with you, Josephina? It was a mere question I'd posed, nothing more."

"I can't," I tried to explain, as horrified as he by my actions. "I don't want to go to London. And you can't come here. You mustn't."

"But I thought—"

"Then you thought wrong."

Not only shock on his face, there were the first stirrings of anger. "I think you might be right. About John. Because you are not kind and sweet. You are…unfeeling."

Unfeeling.

No, no, I am not.

I feel all too keenly.

And those feelings are raw.

Every hour of every day, such feelings are with me. Grey at first but becoming blacker as the day progresses. A cloud that starts to descend from the minute I awake, that refuses to disperse. Only in sleep is there respite. Blessed sleep. A malady, a malaise, one that beauty seems able to mask. An illness becoming more severe. It terrifies me. It mystifies me. Where did it come from? Something so all-encompassing, so powerful.

I couldn't bear the way he was looking at me, the…accusation.

And yet he was right. I was to blame for so much.

Blame that felt like a weight crushing me.

"I'm…so sorry."

Whether he caught my apology, I didn't know. I gathered my skirts, turned from him and ran as fast as I could back inside. Tears streamed down my face. I wiped at them, but they kept coming, a ceaseless well, sobs that erupted as a volcano might, *drawing more attention my way, more eyes filled with surprise, with confusion and horror.*

"Sorry. I am so, so sorry."

Over and over I muttered the same words, like a prayer on my lips.

"Darling?" Mother came towards me, and even though I was an embarrassment, even though I avoided her clasp, was ruining everything, our Christmas party, there was love in her eyes. But so little understanding.

I don't know what happened next, only that the party dispersed. I'd fled to my room, dragged a chest of drawers across the door so that my parents or John couldn't burst in behind me and demand to know what had happened. I fell onto my bed, my hands over my ears to block out any sound other than my own sobbing, and prayed for sleep.

Voices later. Outside my room. Whispers. Only a few words that could be made sense of.

"What...to do... How long...this...on for? Doctors... Try again. Can't... Have to..."

It was my parents, maybe John as well. I closed my eyes and let sleep wash over me.

And now the house is silent, no whispers at all.

I rise from bed and cross over to the window. The night is at its blackest.

For a while I stand here, gazing outwards. Nothing in my mind, just a...vacuum. And then thoughts crowd back. As they always do.

What a disappointment I am.

What a fiend.

A terror.

I am ungrateful.

Selfish.

The devil incarnate.

A burden.

A millstone.

How long could my parents be expected to live with such darkness?

Samuel Marks had a lucky escape.

I freed him, and now I must free those I truly love.

And when they find me, they will ask themselves why. I couldn't be loved any more than I am; the fact I am still at home and not locked away in some terrible institution proves that. And John has spoken so much of me, Samuel said, so highly despite it all.

Why? Why? Why?

Sometimes there is no reason.

The world, such as it is…hurts.

Being here, breathing, hurts.

And sleep is longed for, to end the pain.

I know that what I am about to do will hurt them.

But there is no intention to hurt.

Only a belief that if I am here for longer, it will hurt them more.

Dawn will break soon. Another frosty day. But it is not one that I shall see. And within me, as I pace, there is only relief, a calmness, even, acceptance. It is endless sleep I seek.

Tonight, my card was marked in many ways.

Everything has a time.

And now it is my time.

Why? Why? Why?

Remember this: I have asked that question more than anyone.

Chapter Nineteen

I don't recall having left the chapel – or the sixth bedroom, as I called it – passing my bedroom and returning to hers, Josephina's. But there I was, not standing but sitting slumped against a wall, staring up at a bare light bulb that swayed slightly.

It was quiet. I was cold, and there were tears on my cheeks. I let them fall as I gazed over at the window where Josephina had stood on her last night, unable to bear the oncoming of another day, no matter what day that was or what time of year.

For some, there was no magic, not even at Christmas.

I'm sorry, she had said. *So sorry.* Like a chant, like a litany on her lips. And whenever I had eavesdropped on conversations in my own parents' bedroom, I had heard those same words on my father's lips.

I resented him for what he'd done. I was angry. Furious. For so long rage had simmered beneath the surface, but Carfax House – quiet, lonely Carfax House – by virtue of that same solitude had brought it all crashing to the surface, the *ghost* of Carfax House. Josephina.

Did I hate her too for what she had done so many years ago? Did I blame her? Did I agree with how she'd described herself: a fiend, selfish and a burden?

I shook my head. How could I possibly? I would be the fiend if I did.

"Oh, Josephina," I whispered.

Yes, I had felt bruised and broken, but never had I experienced that degree of hopelessness, that level of bewilderment. Depression could be fuelled by a variety of things – loss, abuse, violence and betrayal – but sometimes…just sometimes, there was no reason other than perhaps a chemical imbalance in the brain. Josephina had had so much to live for, and, in many ways, so had Dad. They'd had people who loved them, who had cared for their wellbeing, who had tried so hard to take care of them and make their world, if not a little brighter, then at least bearable. But sometimes the task was just too great.

There is no intention to hurt. That's what Josephina had said. And yet, inevitably, her actions *would* have hurt others. They would have scarred them, as Dad's actions had scarred Mum and me. Josephina's family would weep and wail, her mother in particular, who'd clearly been as devoted to her as Mum was to Dad, but also her father and John would berate themselves, just as we had done, wondering what more they could have done.

But there was no intention… That was the thing to hold on to, to clutch at when every attempt at applying further logic failed. No one had meant to hurt anyone else.

The world was beautiful, but it was fragile too – and volatile. Often, it was a world of pain.

And some realised that pain; they felt it so deeply.

I'm sorry, she'd said. Dad had been sorry too.

Everything has a time.

Perhaps it was time to accept that apology, to send packing the memory of the man hanging, to remember instead only the time he'd called me princess.

Perhaps it was also time not to banish the memory of Josephina from Carfax House – I couldn't, she was an integral part of it, a woman who had felt so savagely yet was so gentle – but to bring it back to life just as gently. I had a suspicion that since the Standens, no one had loved this house and gardens, not like her mother and father had loved them. It had subsequently been sold on, lived in and sold again, no one ever able to settle. But I could settle, *we* could, me and Al, and any future children, a cat and a dog too. I owed it to her to try. To give love a further chance to heal such sorrow. Because she had done something for me. She had helped me to understand when before I couldn't, shown me her torment in order to set me free of mine.

With that decision made, I remembered what waited downstairs, the mess I'd made.

What time was it?

I still had no idea.

Finally, rising to my feet, I wiped tears from cheeks that were drenched. After one last glance at the window, certain I saw a misty shape there, the merest outline, I left the room and headed towards the staircase, just as she had that night, not sweeping down them in a fancy gown and pearls but tentatively picking my way past all the ruined holly.

Everywhere I looked was debris, Carfax House in a worse state than ever. I didn't survey for too long, however. I headed towards the kitchen to where I'd left my phone.

Switching on the light, I hurried over to it.

So many missed calls, all from Al. Finally, he'd resorted

to texting.

Where are you? Why won't you answer the phone? Maybe it's because the signal's bad, but I'm getting really worried here.

Look, phone me as soon as you can. It was good news! Bloody good news!

Liz? Please phone me. ASAP.

Liz! You are all right, aren't you? You're okay?

Okay, I've checked the train times, and the last one to Leicester has gone. I'd call Shaun or Rob to beg for a lift, but everyone's left, gone home to family already. I'm coming up first thing in the morning, though. Bloody hell, all sorts of scenarios are going through my head! Just let me know you're all right, okay? This silence is killing me!

That last sentence made me smile. He'd said the silence was killing him. I had a counterargument to that. If you listened hard enough, it could deliver you.

I tried returning Al's calls, but the phone went straight to voicemail. I noted the time on the screen. It was so late! 11.59 p.m., and he had started early. No doubt all that alcohol, all that excitement had caught up with him and he was deep in sleep.

One minute to midnight.

I counted down the seconds until midnight arrived.

Christmas Eve.

And then I texted back.

Hey there, sorry about the silence. I've just been so busy and, silly me, let the phone run flat! Anyway, I'm fine, no need to worry. None at all. And don't hurry, your head is bound to be sore in the morning. Catch the lunchtime train. I've got things to do anyway, and I don't want you getting under my feet. I want it to be perfect. You know full well why. It's Christmas, and who goes to as much effort as me at Christmas, huh?!

I can't wait to hear your news. Tell me in person, though, not over the phone. And, Al, I've got something to tell you too. I'm not pregnant, don't worry (!), but it's something I'd like to share. I really am so excited to see you, to welcome you home. It was the right decision to come here. All doubt is gone. We'll be happy here. Really happy.

With the text sent, I then hugged my mobile to me, deciding not to change the ringtone after all. Glancing out of the kitchen window, I noticed something else. It was dark outside, but there was no mist. As if a shroud had been cast aside.

It was Christmas Eve, and Al would be here in a matter of hours.

There was so much work to do, so much to either bin or try to salvage.

And then, as soon as the shops opened, I would rush out to them, be waiting at the door, already bruised credit card in hand, ready to replace all that I had destroyed.

No mean feat, but it was doable. If I put my mind to it.

Which I fully intended to do.

Time and tide waited for no man. And neither did Christmas.

The best thing to do was embrace it.

Chapter Twenty

"Bloody hell, Liz! This is amazing. I really thought, despite what you said in your text last night, that we'd made a big mistake. But no, I love it. Really love it. Look at that staircase! It's fantastic. And the way you've decorated the place. Christ, Liz! I can't tell you how much I love it. How much I appreciate what you've done. This is what I call a homecoming."

Al's delight in turn delighted me. I was glowing, from the tips of my toes to the top of my head. Warmth like a flood coursing through me, my heart leaping in my chest.

God, it had been an effort to get the house to look this way! And I'd barely slept a wink, just an hour shortly before dawn, that's all, and then I was up and at it again, cleaning, baking, uprighting the tree – so glad that the little ballerina in her frosted tutu had survived the onslaught – then making a shopping list crammed with good things.

And all the while, my Roberts radio had been on full blast – a Christmas channel, of course.

As I'd vowed, I was at the shops as soon as they'd opened, having travelled into Birmingham a second time. The cupboards were full, and fresh branches of holly, from the garden this time, were bound to the staircase, their waxy red berries so vibrant.

From the ceiling hung paper snowflakes, stars and even more tinsel than before, and an inflatable snowman *and* an inflatable Father Christmas stood on either side of the door. In what would eventually be a cosy living room complete with a Chesterfield and antique lamps, a fire was roaring, and the lights on the Christmas tree twinkled so merrily.

Al threw his arms around me. "You're incredible, you know that? Forget Christmas, it's you that's the most magical thing ever."

I smiled as I breathed in his clean soap-and-water smell. Pulling apart, I told him he was the incredible one. "You've been made a partner! That's amazing, Al, so amazing."

He didn't disagree. "And, actually, in some ways I'll have more freedom. A bigger workload for sure, but plenty of time to work from home rather than constantly commuting."

"You can go into London as much as you like," I assured him. "I'm fine here."

He raised an eyebrow. "Really? Not afraid of ghosts anymore, then?"

I shook my head. "Not in the least."

What if it's haunted? So many times I'd said that, I'd thought it. And I'd been right – it *was* haunted. If not by an actual presence, by memories just as strong and potent. But I could hardly begrudge Carfax House that, for if it was haunted, then so was I. Again, by memories I couldn't shrug off but which now I'd at least come to understand and accept. Some people couldn't live, no matter how much those around them might wish they could. We could get angry about it, we could cry and yell in frustration, take them by the shoulders and shake them, but it would make no difference. Yet there *was* something that made a difference. At least for those left behind. It was living for them, those of us that could. It was taking a moment to stop and smell the roses, to note how blue the sky was and how green the grass. It was realising you couldn't be happy all the time, that no one ever was. Giving yourself a break when anger resurfaced, when sadness set in. Shit happened. But it would pass, if you let it.

John talked of the lights in London, electric lights, introduced around the late 1800s, and Josephina had wondered at it. She'd never got to see those lights, but, hopefully, somewhere the light was waiting for her. She and Dad and so many.

Al didn't know about the grave in the garden. I'd tell him soon. First, though, I had to tell him the truth about my father, tonight, perhaps, over a glass or two of wine. Why wait any longer? It was a secret but not a dirty one. The real disservice was having told Al a lie.

We completed a tour of the house, Al's eyes as wide as could be every step of the way, especially when we approached the old oak door in the sixth bedroom, when I grabbed that big iron ring and pushed it open to reveal the chapel.

"Good God!" he said, and I laughed.

"Don't take the Lord's name in vain."

"But what's that doing here? It wasn't on the details."

"No, it wasn't, but I rather like it. It's…quirky."

"Damn right it is. Not sure it's going to stay, though."

"Oh, it is," I insisted. "It's what you call an original feature. We can send the kids here in the future to do penance. It'll be like a glorified naughty step."

"Hmm," was Al's response. "I'm still thinking a walk-in wardrobe's a better bet."

"No. It's special. It's staying."

We returned downstairs, and I sat Al down in the living room while I rushed through to the kitchen to fetch the biscuits I'd made and the wine.

"You really are spoiling me," he said upon my return, "you know that? And you iced the biscuits, little snowmen."

I pointed to another. "And reindeer too. And Father Christmas."

Al frowned. "That's Father Christmas, is it? I was wondering."

"Hey," I said, shoving him. "Perhaps I was never quite as good at drawing as writing, but at least I tried."

"Can't argue with that," he said, pulling me into his arms.

Was now the time to ask?

To be fair, I had *already* asked. Just not him.

"Al, tonight is ours, Christmas Eve, but tomorrow, well…tomorrow, Christmas Day, how d'you feel if we had a guest?"

He pulled away from me. "A guest? What do you mean?"

"I've met someone."

"What?" His expression was comical! "Who?"

I explained then about Patricia and how she'd be alone on Christmas Day. That I'd phoned her to see if she'd like to join us for dinner, offering to fetch and take her back.

She'd been delighted, over the moon, kept asking if I was certain, if she wouldn't be imposing.

"Al?" I said, having given him enough time to mull over

the idea. "I mean, if you'd rather we didn't, I could phone her again. Perhaps suggest Boxing Day instead. I'm sorry. I should have discussed it first with you. I didn't mean to ruin things."

"Ruin things? You haven't. Don't think that, Liz, not for a second. No, I agree, it was the right thing to do, asking her." A smile wiped away any further bafflement. "No one should be alone at Christmas," he said, reminding me of how much I loved him and how bright our future could be.

* * *

Dinner was done, and it was a triumph, even if I say so myself.

The turkey was roasted to perfection; the stuffing was herby enough; the roast potatoes zinged with rosemary, sage and garlic; and the carrots had that lovely honey tang.

Al, Patricia and I had sat around the table in the kitchen, the heating behaving itself for once, chatting, pulling crackers and eating our fill. With plates now empty, we reclined in our chairs, Al's party hat slightly lopsided, holding our sides and moaning that we should have perhaps exercised a little restraint. On Al's wrist was the watch I'd bought him, which he loved. He'd bought me an antique diamond pendant on a necklace that I was also wearing, one hand lifting up at regular intervals just so I could feel it, a stone that dazzled.

I'd also got Patricia some gifts, token gestures, really – some toiletries, a pair of pale blue cashmere socks and a posh box of chocolates – and she'd been delighted with them. She'd already had a FaceTime chat with her daughter, son-in-law and grandchild this morning. Christmas Day was almost over for them by then, but we still had ours.

Al suggested a game of cards, so I cleared the table whilst he went to fetch the pack, which I'd told him I'd placed in a drawer in the scullery.

A lovely day so far, it was everything I wanted it to be.

Al knew about my father now. I'd cried when telling him, and he had held me. Yes, he'd been shocked, but more so because I'd kept it from him.

"There's no need to be ashamed," he'd said, and I reminded him I wasn't, not anymore. I would tell him the rest – about Josephina, her grave and what had happened at Carfax House during his absence – but one thing at a time, get him used to living here first, just as I'd got used to it. I'd had a crash course!

It was whilst we were playing cards that Patricia paused, one hand about to lay a card but suspended in midair instead.

"Is everything all right?" Al asked her.

"Yes," she said. "I think so."

His eyes remained on her.

I knew what she was doing; she was listening.

"It sounds like…there's someone pacing upstairs," she said eventually.

Al also inclined his head. "Does it? Oh, hang on. Maybe." He then looked at me quizzically. "What do you think it could be?"

I shrugged. "That," I replied, smiling widely, "be the ghost of Carfax House."

"Ooh, aargh!" Al's tone was just as jovial. "We're haunted

after all!"

Seeing Patricia's slight look of alarm, I quickly reassured her. "Houses make strange noises all the time, don't they? It's nothing, creaky floorboards."

A memory.

Reaching for my glass, which was filled with sparkling water rather than wine, being as I had to drive later, I lifted it high. "Let's raise a toast," I said. "To Carfax House. To friends, both old and new. To family, both near and far. Merry Christmas."

"Merry Christmas," Patricia responded, lifting her glass and clinking it against mine.

"Merry Christmas." Al clinked glasses as well.

"Let there be peace on earth," I added.

And peace in the heavens too.

A note from the author

As much as I love writing, building a relationship with readers is even more exciting! I occasionally send newsletters with details on new releases, special offers and other bits of news relating to the Psychic Surveys series as well as all my other books. If you'd like to subscribe, sign up here!

www.shanistruthers.com

Printed in Great Britain
by Amazon